THE PEOPLE'S
CARDINAL

HARRY L. SHEEHY

The characters in this novel are fictitious, and any resemblance between them and any persons living or dead is purely coincidental.

~

ISBN-10: 0692229396
ISBN-13: 978-0692229392

To my wife Carolyn,
for her unstinting support,
her insightful critique,
her editorial contributions.

~

PROLOGUE

April 2040

Christian Bauer returned to his residence in the Parioli section of Rome after a particularly busy day at the Vatican. Cardinal Bauer was returning from a long session briefing the new Pope – Paul VII, elected March 7, 2040 – about recurring issues at the Congregation for the Doctrine of the Faith.

He opened his front door to a vestibule leading to his study, and noticed a bottle in gift wrap sitting on his desk at the opposite side of the large room. It had not been there when he left for the papal apartments in the morning.

Our doorman must have accepted this for me, and brought it up so I'd have it when I came home.

He locked the door behind him, entered his study and crossed the room to his desk. Next to the bottle was an unsigned note that read: "To Cardinal Bauer, a small recognition of the service you have rendered to all the bishops in your important curial role."

What a nice gesture, Bauer thought as he unwrapped the bottle.

It was his favorite, a dark Spanish sherry, a glass of which he always enjoyed before his evening meal. Three cardinals had joined him for a drink the evening before, prior to dinner at his favorite trattoria: Dieter Kaufmann, Archbishop of Munich, his home diocese; and two Curia officials – Antonio Ruggieri and Flavio Scarpelli.

They emptied my bottle, knowing it was my last. This gift must be from one of them.

At 9:00 p.m. he poured himself a glass and sat on his sofa to read and relax before preparing a late supper.

Fifteen minutes later, his phone rang. Bauer did not answer the phone. He slumped against the arm of the sofa, book on his lap and reading glasses cocked crookedly on his nose. A moment later a loud knock sounded on his door. Bauer never stirred.

A key turned in the door lock, and a darkly clothed figure entered the study and crossed the room. He removed a syringe from his briefcase, attached a hypodermic needle, and injected the syringe's contents into the slumbering Bauer.

He picked up the sherry bottle and the partially consumed glass of sherry, drained the bottle into the sink, and placed the empty bottle in his briefcase. He washed and dried the sherry glass, wiping it clean of any finger prints.

He returned to the unconscious Bauer, removed a pistol from his case, attached a silencer, and fired a single shot into the Cardinal's heart.

The assailant went to Bauer's desk, opened the file drawer, and rummaged through the contents, clearly looking for something, tossing everything on the floor until he found the object of his search.

Putting that in his briefcase, he returned to the vestibule, let himself out, relocked the door and checked his watch. He accomplished his mission in under 10 minutes.

CHAPTER 1

The month was August, the year 2045. Cardinal Albert Rooney was on his way to O'Hare International Airport to board a flight to Rome. Everything was in order, he was sure. His secretary and assistant, Father Carl Roszak, had seen to it that the things he needed for an extended stay in Rome were packed: his suitcase with personal belongings; his briefcase with notes and short vignettes he had written just in case he was asked to make a presentation; his file containing important statistics on the health and progress – or lack thereof – of the Chicago Archdiocese.

This was not Rooney's first trip to Vatican City since becoming Archbishop of Chicago two years before. He traveled there a year ago to receive his cardinal's red hat from the late Pope Paul VII. Today's trip was less propitious; he was traveling to attend the funeral of the same Pope and to participate in the Conclave of cardinals that would elect the new leader of the Roman Catholic Church.

Before leaving for the airport, Cardinal Rooney phoned David McLaughlin, Cardinal Archbishop of New York, a good friend with whom he had worked closely at the USCCB – the U.S. Conference of Catholic Bishops. When Rooney was a newly ordained bishop and unfamiliar with the USCCB protocols, McLaughlin had taken him under his wing – acted as Rooney's mentor. McLaughlin was already in Rome, having left the U.S. three days earlier.

"David, you attended the funeral of Leo XIV and participated in the Conclave that elected Paul VII," Rooney said. "I did not. I am a little worried about maintaining proper protocol. Do you have a moment for a couple of questions?"

Albert Rooney was always concerned with appearances, never wanting to embarrass himself. Cardinal McLaughlin did his best to set Rooney's mind at ease.

"When you get to Rome you will receive a booklet prepared by the Camerlengo – the papal chamberlain – with all the protocols for the time following the death of a pope. Everything you need to know will be in there."

As his plane lifted off the tarmac at O'Hare and set its course for Rome, Rooney's emotions ran the gamut of sadness over the death of the Pope, humility in the face of the overwhelming responsibility to select the next pope, and a certain excitement to be part of such an important historic occasion.

Events now destined to unfold would indeed make church history.

CHAPTER 2

Few officials in the Roman Catholic Church could match the laser-like focus and bulldog tenacity of Cardinal Antonio Ruggieri. When he set his sights on a particular goal, nothing in heaven or on earth was likely to stop him. Few– if any – who knew this man had the temerity to get in his way once he made up his mind to achieve an objective.

As required of all principal curial officials, Ruggieri had resigned his post as Prefect of the Congregation for the Doctrine of the Faith when Paul VII died. Years before, he had filled this position under Gregory XVII, but lost it when Leo XIV appointed Christian Bauer in his stead. Upon Bauer's death, Paul VII turned to him to once again to assume the powerful post.

On the eve of Paul VII's funeral, Ruggieri invited his closest associates – certain curial officials and a few cardinal archbishops in Rome for the funeral and subsequent Conclave – to a meeting at his residence. His manner was stern, even grim. Ruggieri was hell-bent on accomplishing something, and demanded their cooperation.

"The Church is in crisis," he harangued, "and it's our duty to take aggressive action. The 21st century popes have let Church discipline slowly slip away, and ever so slowly lose its power and authority over the laity."

"It's the 'sausage game,' you know – you cut one small slice of the sausage, and it's hardly noticeable. Then, another slice, and another. Finally you're left with nothing in your hand but the string!"

Cardinal Angelo Molinaro, Prefect of the Congregation for Bishops, chimed in.

"There are over two hundred prelates in the College of Cardinals now, Antonio. Surely among them are many suitable candidates to be the. . ."

Ruggieri interrupted him abruptly and continued.

"The Church has never been more in need of a strong leader. I'm not talking about a globetrotting celebrity. I'm not talking about a media savvy, baby-kissing pontiff who spits out clever sound bites. We've had all that, haven't we? And where has it gotten us? The Church has never found itself in such dire straits."

"I'm talking about a leader who has backbone – has guts. A man who is not afraid of public opinion or of ruffling feathers, who will bring Holy Mother Church back to the purity and discipline that has been its hallmark over the millennia."

There was no doubt in the mind of anyone in the room about whom Cardinal Antonio Ruggieri was talking. He expected those present to elect him the next Bishop of Rome in the coming Conclave. His ambition knew no bounds. For this very reason, Cardinals who knew him, and most did, rightfully feared what might happen if Ruggieri gained more power than he already had. The probability of his being selected pope was just short of nil.

CHAPTER 3

The 10-hour flight to Rome was almost over as the plane descended over the northeast shore of the Mediterranean and approached da Vinci International Airport. As the plane banked for its landing, Cardinal Rooney could see the dome of St. Peter's Basilica at the Vatican, dominating the skyline of Rome.

Vatican City is an anomaly, he thought.

This small piece of real estate, surrounded by the city of Rome and occupying just 109 acres on the west side of the Tiber River, is home to the smallest state in the world – smaller even than Monaco, San Marino, or Liechtenstein.

And yet, its government, the Holy See, with the pope at its head, has a greater impact on the world we live in than nations many times its size. What better example is there than how it influenced the collapse of Soviet communism in the late 20th century?

In a matter of days, Albert Rooney would be casting his vote for the next leader of the Holy See and the worldwide Catholic Church.

Cardinal Rooney checked in at the Hilton Garden Inn, in the heart of Rome. He went to St. Peter's Basilica that evening to view Paul VII's body lying in state, and to pray.

When he returned to the hotel he ran into Cardinal McLaughlin, who was also staying at the Hilton. They retired to the hotel lounge to chat, and enjoy a nightcap.

"Albert, good to see you," McLaughlin stated warmly, as he took a sip of his Brandy Alexander, "although I wish it were for a happier occasion. Paul VII was a good man, a holy man, but he was overwhelmed by the challenges these days. A heart attack, they say. I have to believe it was the insurmountable problems facing the Church that broke his heart, and brought an end to his life."

Rooney responded: "A remarkable man. I wish I had known him better."

"I got here three days ago," McLaughlin continued, "and have talked to many of the cardinals I know regarding who may be the best candidates. Very few names come up. Those that do are not considered realistic possibilities, even some . . ."

McLaughlin shuddered involuntarily.

"Think of the problems we are facing now, Albert. The laity is eroding before our eyes, and too many people who call themselves Catholics are effectively truant most of the time. The last three popes have tried, but failed to find a solution."

"Some people only show up at church to be 'hatched, matched and dispatched,'" Rooney commented. "The financial support we came to expect from the laity has dwindled to a trickle. In Chicago, we're selling our nonessential real estate to make ends meet. I am sure you face the same thing in New York."

"The financial problems are ubiquitous," McLaughlin agreed, "even at the Holy See. Fiscal pain is crippling us at all levels."

Albert Rooney stirred his Whiskey Sour with a swivel stick, and took a sip.

"Then there's the downturn in vocations to the priesthood," he noted, "and a disturbing number of young priests have left to get married."

"It is a disaster, Albert, and no one's got the magic wand to set it right. Who, in his right mind, would want to become Supreme Pontiff and assume responsibility for these problems? We could go on and on – women's ordination, abortion, same-sex marriage, reforming the governance of the Church. The challenges are overwhelming."

Albert Rooney and David McLaughlin ended their conversation in a shared moment of gloom, and bid each other goodnight. While they had hit on the key issues facing the Catholic Church, neither had any realization that a much deeper problem for the Church loomed on the horizon.

CHAPTER 4

Not visually striking, Rooney could melt into any crowd unnoticed—never mind a sea of cardinals. At 63, with his 5'8" frame carrying about 20 pounds more than he needed, and his non-descript square face framed by silver colored wire-frame glasses, head mostly bald, with just a fringe of gray hair around his temples, he hardly radiated the image you might expect from one of the Church's preeminent prelates.

An ambitious man, he saw himself heading one of the more prestigious departments of the Roman Curia someday, and he especially wanted to make a favorable impression on those cardinals with curial positions.

The Rooneys were no strangers to ambition. His father and grandfather were respected lawyers, civic leaders, politicians even. His father was a prominent alderman who went on to serve as a state representative for Chicago's Bridgeport neighborhood.

"Do you realize how far this family has come?" his father never hesitated to remind Albert when he was young. "Our ancestors immigrated from County Down to escape the Great Famine in 1847. They broke their backs on the Illinois & Michigan Canal, and worked in the stockyards for pennies an hour. Your grandfather and I were the first to get an education, and look what we made of ourselves by studying the law! You ought to do the same."

"I'll be important, Dad, but in my own way," young Albert invariably responded.

A priest on the faculty of the De La Salle Institute where he attended high school, inspired him to consider a vocation to the priesthood.

"You're a pious and ethical lad," the clergyman would tell him, "and you're a top-notch student. The priesthood needs men like you, Albert. Think about it, pray about it – God may be calling you. Pay attention to His promptings! As you pray with your lips, boy, listen with your heart and soul!"

Upon graduation, Albert entered the junior seminary at Niles, and then the major seminary at Mundelein.

Since before the turn of the century, many young men entering the seminary – perhaps a majority – were conservative and traditional in their practice of Catholicism, and felt the liberalizing reforms promulgated by the Second Vatican Council in the mid-20th century were at best ill-advised, if not downright un-Catholic.

Albert Rooney was fully in accord with this thinking, and never hesitated to make his views known. He invariably made a favorable impression on the hierarchy and seminary staff, who largely shared his ideas.

Prior to his ordination, like many who showed promise, and curried favor with their superiors, Albert was sent to Rome for studies in theology at the Gregorian University. He saw a bright future for himself.

My father always said Rooneys are destined to be leaders in their professional undertakings. I will be no exception to that tradition.

After ordination, he climbed the rungs in Chicago, first as an associate pastor, then pastor, and at only 35 years of age, an auxiliary bishop in the archdiocese of St. Louis—the youngest in the United States. His career as a Church prelate was launched. If Albert Rooney learned nothing else from his father, he learned how to get ahead.

After his success in St. Louis, he was appointed Archbishop of Kansas City, and, on the day before his sixty-first birthday, Archbishop of Chicago. One year later, Pope Paul VII presented Albert Rooney with a cardinal's red biretta.

Flying to Rome, Rooney reflected on the fact that more than a hundred cardinals of the Church would congregate at Vatican City to carry out the awesome responsibility of selecting a new leader of one of the world's great religions at a crucial moment in the life of the Church.

He and his colleagues, unbeknownst to them all, were about to drastically alter the direction of the Church.

CHAPTER 5

Two days after Cardinal Rooney's arrival in Rome, tens of thousands of the faithful packed Saint Peter's Square for the funeral Mass on the steps of the Basilica, in front of Maderno's splendid façade. Astride the altar were seats for cardinals, the hierarchy of eastern Rite churches, prominent Protestant clergy, heads of state and representatives from countries around the world. Among their number were four kings, three queens, seventy-seven presidents and prime ministers and a score of leaders of the world's great religions. Cardinal Albert Rooney, Archbishop of Chicago, took his place among them.

In front of the altar rested the casket of Paul VII.

The significance of what was to transpire during the next few days was very much on Rooney's mind.

This starts my participation in the most important event in my life. It surely will affect the future of the Church, and forever impact my life as well.

He had no real conception of how true that would prove to be.

Federico Lanzillo, the Dean of the College of Cardinals, presided at the funeral Mass, wearing a red chasuble with intricate embroidery. Eight score of cardinals surrounding the altar were also vested with red chasubles, but without the elaborate needlework enhancements. Lanzillo and the other cardinals wore white miters on their heads, the miter a symbol of their leadership role as bishops, the unadorned color white a tradition at funerals.

After the reading of the Gospel, Cardinal Lanzillo stood before the congregation to offer his homily. He greeted the heads of state and dignitaries present, and the religious leaders and representatives from around the world in attendance for this solemn occasion.

Cardinal Lanzillo told the story of Paul VII's early years, his vocation to the priesthood, his significant accomplishments as a member of the Holy See's diplomatic corps, and his substantial achievements as Supreme Pontiff. He underscored Paul's challenges as Pope:

"No pope this century, or in any century, has faced as many challenges as our beloved Paul VII. During his all-too-brief pontificate, he had to exercise moral leadership for the Catholic Church in a world that has been secularized by a faltering ethical compass.

"This was a man for all seasons, who dedicated himself to making the world a better place, in which every one of God's children might live to their fullest possibilities under the provenance of their divine Creator.

"Paul not only dedicated himself to the welfare of the Church, but was a strong advocate of environmental issues, and of world peace. Following St. Paul's lead in First Corinthians, Pope Paul VII strove to be 'all things to all men.' His agenda was ambitious. Though his Creator deigned to take him before he completed it, we thank God we enjoyed his leadership for at least a few short years."

It was a gorgeous August day. The haunting choral music and the words of praise in Cardinal Lanzillo's homily made an ideal send-off for the deceased Pope.

Many of the cardinals were genuinely sorry to see the demise of Paul VII, and worried who might fill his shoes, who might bring his plans to fruition.

Others welcomed the opportunity his death presented, to find a successor who would dismantle what Paul had endeavored to achieve, and bring the Church back to an earlier time – an era of a more disciplined and authoritarian way of doing things. A time when the clergy, the select, the chosen, rightfully ran the show. No one welcomed that opportunity more keenly than Cardinal Antonio Ruggieri.

CHAPTER 6

"We haven't got much time, Dieter. The stakes couldn't be higher. This is probably our last opportunity to make a difference – a big difference!"

Antonio Ruggieri paced back and forth in his large office at the Congregation for the Doctrine of the Faith, occasionally throwing up his arms above his head in a gesture of frustration. Seated on a sofa across the room was Dieter Kaufmann, Cardinal Archbishop of Munich.

Ruggieri and Kaufmann had been classmates at the Pontifical Lateran University, and in the early years, their advancement as minor Curia bureaucrats had followed virtually parallel tracks. They had similar high ambitions for their careers, and both faithfully subscribed to the maxim that the end justifies the means.

After Ruggieri became a prefect, he was instrumental in getting Kaufmann appointed Archbishop of Munich, and hoped to eventually see him back in Rome as prefect of a curial congregation. Dieter Kaufmann was aware his aspirations were closely connected to the successful fulfillment of Antonio Ruggieri's ambition.

That ambition, Kaufmann was well aware, was to ascend to the highest office in the Roman Catholic Church – to become pope.

"You know, Antonio, I wouldn't suggest that you openly lobby for votes in the upcoming Conclave. Since that's not considered acceptable, I feel certain it would backfire."

"There are only a dozen Cardinals whom I can count on to cast their votes for me," Ruggieri acknowledged reluctantly. "There must be a way we can make more of them understand that I am the best hope the Church has to bring it back to its pristine strength – to restore its purity."

Cardinal Kaufman rubbed his chin and said, "There will be speakers at the General Congregation preceding the Conclave, some appointed by Lanzillo. You need to request he appoint some who shares our traditional Catholic values.

"We need a new voice," Kaufmann continued, "an important figure whose views are orthodox, but who has not as yet had much exposure at the Vatican."

"I know just such a figure, " Ruggieri interjected, "he's perfect. He heads the second largest archdiocese in the U.S., and has been a cardinal for less than a year. He's considered an articulate speaker, one of the most conservative voices in the American hierarchy."

"I will ask Lanzillo to tap Albert Rooney as one of the speakers."

CHAPTER 7

"Cardinal Rooney, this is Cardinal Lanzillo," the voice on the other end of the phone announced.

"I am pleased to tell you Cardinal Antonio Ruggieri has recommended that you be one of the speakers at the General Congregation."

"Cardinal Ruggieri, did you say, the Prefect of the Congregation for the Doctrine of the Faith? I am flattered, but why would he possibly recommend me?"

"It's clear you don't know Ruggieri," Lanzillo responded in a somewhat patronizing tone. "He hears everything, sees everything. Your reputation as an articulate traditionalist and spokesman of the American church is well-known to him. He believes your orthodox views can contribute to this gathering of cardinals."

Rooney was delighted. He smiled, and felt very smug.

This will give me considerable exposure, and ultimately contribute to my appointment to a Vatican commission or congregation. No question I was wise to pack my presentation notes.

The period of mourning now over, the General Congregation was scheduled to begin, a meeting of several days which all cardinals eligible to vote for the next pope were required to attend. Its purpose was to set a date for the papal election Conclave, and to discuss the daunting issues facing the Church, issues the new pope must surely deal with – issues that would influence his selection.

The General Congregation commenced the following day. A number of cardinals were slated to address the General Congregation. Two speakers preceded Albert Rooney, saying almost nothing new or revelatory.

Cardinal Rooney then rose to address the assembly. He began, like the first two, by first eulogizing Paul VII, and underscoring the misfortune of having him depart this life with so much of his agenda left incomplete. He then went on:

"It is clear that ever since the unfortunate relaxation – not just relaxation, but elimination – of time-honored traditions and religious disciplines as a result of Vatican II, many of the laity have gone astray, substituting secular licentious and materialistic standards for a life properly sanctified through the guidance of the Church."

He described, in detail, several of the ascetical practices and inflexible regulations that were prevalent 100 years before, but were abandoned in the wake of Vatican II – practices and regulations, he insisted, essential to humanity's quest for eternal salvation.

"My brothers in Christ, it is we few, the successors of the apostles, who have been given the extraordinary mission to be custodians of the faith, to scrutinize how far the faithful have deviated from the dictates of the Gospel and the magisterium of the Church, and to correct and restore our one, holy, Catholic and apostolic faith."

As Cardinal Rooney took his seat, there was a low-level murmuring, as the prelates reacted with surprise at the tenor of his remarks. He was clearly ultraconservative. Most of his brethren, though conservative, were less inclined to go as far as he did in advocating a return to earlier times.

During the daily coffee breaks, Albert Rooney made it a point to meet cardinals he didn't know. Most of them were politely complimentary about the address he had given, but didn't show any sign of real support.

Finally he approached Cardinal Ruggieri, who expressed genuine enthusiasm for Rooney's point-of-view.

"It was a great honor to be asked to speak," Rooney responded sincerely, "I don't know how I can thank you for nominating me"

"Too many of us," Ruggieri observed, "have become virtually anesthetized by modernism, insensitive to the gradual and insidious transfusion of materialism into the veins of the Church."

"During my two years shepherding the Chicago Church," Rooney added, "I have become all too aware of this, and it deeply concerns me. It is pervasive in my Archdiocese, and I intend to do all I can to stem it."

Ruggieri noted: "It is imperative we select a pontiff who will reverse the prevailing trends and bring us back to the Church's true mission."

At the coffee breaks, almost no names emerged of any cardinals who were "papabile," who could fill "the Shoes of the Fisherman" and successfully address the current challenges facing the Church. The discussions were often oblique, since it was not acceptable for any Cardinal to campaign for the Church's supreme position; and if a Cardinal was told that he would be an ideal pope, he was expected only to say he was not worthy. Anyone eavesdropping on informal discussions could hear comments such as:

> "How can it be that, during this century, our problems not only haven't been solved, but have actually gotten worse?"

> "Why does the rare qualified candidate for this high office say, if offered the challenge, he will refuse to accept it?"

> "Who among us can and will give to the Church the leadership it needs now?"

The General Congregation dragged on for five days, and on the eve of the Conclave, the mood was sullen. No one seemed clear on how they would get from Point A to Point B.

Little did they realize they were about to set in motion one of the most significant innovations in many centuries, and lay the seeds for a crisis that would shake the Church to its very foundations.

CHAPTER 8

Father William Bracey sat staring at the picture of St. Ignatius on the wall, trying to make sense of this call. In itself, there was nothing unusual about hearing from Stefano Paganelli, the senior Cardinal Bishop. Ever since Father Bracey had come to Rome four years ago, he and Cardinal Paganelli had occasion for frequent contact, and had developed a real friendship.

This call, however, was unique, and very strange. The College of Cardinals was in their General Congregation in preparation for the papal election. Although they weren't yet *cum clave*, literally locked in with a key at the Conclave, they were not supposed to attend to any unrelated matters at this time.

"Father Bracey, I may need to see you shortly. I hope you have no plans to be out of Rome in the next few days."

"I was planning to visit our Madrid provincial headquarters, your Eminence, but that can be postponed. Can you tell me what this is about?"

"All I can say, at this time, is that there is a matter of some urgency, and your involvement may be of considerable importance," the Cardinal replied. "Please remain available. I must go now, but we will speak again soon," he concluded, hanging up abruptly and cutting off any opportunity for Bracey to ask further questions.

Bracey had no idea what was on Paganelli's mind, but knew a man in his position wouldn't have made such a request casually.

He decided to remain in Rome until he had a chance to talk at length with the Cardinal. He would stay until after the new pope was elected.

***

For five centuries, since the founding of the Society of Jesus in 1540, Jesuit Superior Generals have been close confidants of the pope. Their traditional black cassocks, and the pontiff's willingness to lend them an ear, long ago earned them the nickname "black pope." Cardinal Paganelli frequently served as the conduit between Paul VII and Father Bracey, and sometimes served as a third person in their discussions.

William Bracey's path to the top job in the Society of Jesus was anything but typical, and certainly not predictable.

In the late 20th century his family immigrated from Poland, and settled in Merced, California. His father felt their surname, Abramowicz, was too foreign and probably too Jewish-sounding for Merced, so they anglicized it to Bracey. He also changed his three-year old son's name from Velvel bar-Moshe to William, the English equivalent of the Yiddish Velvel.

His father was very old country in his thinking and actions, but William was entirely a contemporary American boy. Bracey senior, owner of a hardware store, was observant, and maintained the Jewish traditions. He and his wife kept a kosher home. A change in name in no way affected his Jewish identity.

Merced had a relatively small Jewish population, William had very few Jewish friends, and he grew away from the faith, identifying more closely with his gentile friends. As a matter of fact, William really didn't identify with any faith tradition at all.

"We have customs handed down to us from the time God made us the Chosen People," his father would remind William. "They are important – they define who we are. You cause me great sadness when you ignore the traditions that strengthen us, identify us, tie us closer to our Creator."

"They make us different, Papa – they make us stand out," William typically retorted. "Maybe they were fine in Poland, but not here. I have no friends who go to synagogue on the Sabbath, or wear a yarmulke. It makes me feel strange."

"It makes you a real Jew, William," his father replied. "We are not *goyem*. We have a deep religious heritage, an older heritage, a proud heritage. You should accept it, and hold your head up high."

Friday evening Shabbat dinner was often an issue, especially in the fall when William's high school had a Friday night football game. William wouldn't show up for dinner. His father was usually furious.

"William is almost a man now," his mother would counsel her husband. "He must make his own decisions on how he lives."

"It is hard to believe this son of mine, who had his Bar Mitzvah last year, would prove himself to be so irreverent," his father lamented. "What will ever become of him?"

CHAPTER 9

In his senior year of high school, William applied to the University of San Francisco, a Jesuit college. He was bright, had good grades, and USF offered him a generous scholarship. This, plus the fact that living in San Francisco really appealed to him, brought him to the Bay Area.

As he expected, he excelled academically at USF. What he didn't anticipate was a growing curiosity about religion which he had not experienced before.

Other than my own family, I've never seen so many people who are into religion, he mused. *There's something there, but I don't get what the attraction is.*

William's freshman class was multi-cultural, multi-racial and multi-religious. Catholics predominated and some of them turned out to be his best friends. They talked religion, and he was fascinated by the role their faith played in their lives, and perhaps a little jealous – he sensed they had something he didn't have, something that was important.

In the spring of his first year, the student calendar included a three-day retreat for those freshmen who were interested, at El Retiro San Iñigo, the Jesuit Retreat Center in Los Altos.

"As you probably know, in two weeks the annual freshmen retreat is scheduled at El Retiro," one of his good friends said to him. "Some of us are going. Care to join us?"

"I don't think so," William replied. "I'm not a Catholic. I'm not even religious. Those three days would be a waste of my time, I'm afraid."

"You don't have to be a Catholic," his friend told him. "Lots of non-Catholics and non-Christians go there. It's a chance to reflect on where you've been and where you're going, something we don't take time to do when we've got calculus problems to solve, essays to write and term paper deadlines. All that stuff stops for three whole days. It's pretty cool. It's a time away we can all use."

William signed on.

The Spiritual Exercises of St. Ignatius, the presentations by the retreat director, his reflective walks alone in the foothills of the Santa Cruz Mountains – the retreat was a veritable epiphany for William Bracey. He was being exposed to something – something he wanted – missing from his life, and having it now became a priority.

Events triggered by the three days at El Retiro San Iñigo moved rapidly. He joined the Catholic Church that summer, and before the year was through, he decided to become a Jesuit priest. He entered the Jesuit novitiate the next fall.

***

After his ordination, Father William Bracey earned an MBA at Harvard, and a PhD in philosophy at Stanford. Over the next few years, he enjoyed a quick ascent through a variety of substantial assignments: high school principal, rector of a Jesuit novitiate, college president, and finally Provincial of the Society of Jesus USA West Province.

He was noted for being a good administrator, a problem solver, and a very effective leader who could draw consensus from widely diverse points of view. Contributing to his widely recognized leadership qualities was his commanding physical presence – six feet tall, trim, strong clef chin, black wavy hair slightly graying at the temples and piercing blue eyes. His gait was paced and deliberate, never hurried, almost regal with shoulders held back, posture erect. One of his colleagues said of him: "When you're with William Bracey, you *really* know you're with someone special!"

In 2041, Father Bracey was a representative at the Jesuit General Congregation in Rome to elect a new Superior General for the Order. This 49 year-old American Provincial knew he was considered a strong candidate for this position, but his election on the first ballet came as a complete surprise.

His team-building and problem-solving abilities were tested fairly frequently in his position as Superior General, and his ability for effective leadership, along with his dedication to the Church, were generally recognized by a number of significant officials at the Vatican.

William Bracey epitomized the standard set by St. Ignatius, a man with a military background, who declared that the Society of Jesus was founded for "whoever desires to serve as a soldier of God."

Although Jesuits are mostly noted for their intellectual activities in high schools, colleges and universities, and pastoral ministries in parishes, hospitals and retreat houses, they are expected to go, like good soldiers, wherever the Church needs their services.

Throughout his calling as a Jesuit, William Bracey did whatever he was asked to do, and went wherever he was sent, fulfilling the demanding Ignatian standard to the letter.

CHAPTER 10

The General Congregation concluded with the vast majority of Cardinals dissatisfied with everyone in the small field of possible candidates for pope.

Cardinal Ruggieri was not part of that majority. The Prefect of the Congregation for the Doctrine of the Faith knew exactly who could do the job now required, who could make the hard decisions necessary to bring the faithful back to the age-old disciplines and practices which were the hallmarks of the Church.

When they elect me, we will put an end to the disgraceful laissez faire approach to religion which is eating away the very fabric of the Church.

He could count on the backing of a small, loyal cohort of cardinals.

The following day, after the celebration of Mass in St. Peter's Basilica, the cardinals, two-by-two, resplendent in their red cassocks, matching birettas and white lace-trimmed surplices, processed from the Pauline Chapel in the Vatican Palace to the Sistine Chapel as they sang the *Veni Creator Spiritus.*

After all were assembled in this magnificent edifice with Raphael's tapestries on the side walls, hung especially for this occasion, and Michelangelo's resplendent frescos on the ceiling and wall behind the altar, the Dean of the College of Cardinals, Federico Lanzillo, read the oath they must take:

- *if elected, to defend the freedom of the Holy See;*

- *to vote honestly for whom they feel is the best choice;*

- *to maintain total secrecy regarding the proceedings of the Conclave.*

Each cardinal, in succession, placed his hand on the Bible, and swore to uphold this sacred oath. Anyone ineligible to vote or who was not otherwise authorized to remain was ordered to leave by the Master of the Papal Liturgical Celebrations. He then closed and sealed the door.

During the Conclave, two votes are taken each morning, and two each afternoon. After each vote, the ballots are burned in a special stove installed in the Sistine Chapel for this sole purpose, with the chimney reaching high above the Chapel roof. If no one receives two-thirds of the votes cast, a substance is added to the burning ballots that blackens the rising smoke to tell the waiting world no pope has yet been chosen. However, if a pope is elected, an added substance makes the smoke white, and the bells of St. Peter's Basilica begin to peal.

The voting began. When the first votes were tallied, there were 15 different cardinals that were voted for, with the votes fairly evenly distributed – a clear sign no consensus existed.

Subsequent ballots were taken with the same results. Although what goes on in Conclaves is secret, and no one knew what past Conclaves had done, a general feeling among the participants was that these results were unprecedented in recent times.

Cardinal Ruggieri consistently voted for himself, and a few other ultra-conservative prelates supported him. The majority of cardinals, however, did not consider him a viable candidate, even for a minute.

Most cardinals who knew Antonio Ruggieri were justifiably concerned about what would happen if this man became too powerful.

They did not trust him. But he did have followers, a group of Cardinals firmly under his thumb, a clique that helped him reach his goals.

Despite his early failure to achieve a majority of votes, Ruggieri still displayed an over-bounding confidence and strong ego.

If this voting goes on long enough, the other electors will recognize I am the best hope for steering the Church on a straight course from this point on.

The Conclave procedure dictated that, after three days of unsuccessful voting, the process be suspended for a maximum of one day. During this time, the senior Cardinal Deacon is required to address the assembly, urging them to consider what is truly needed by the Church at this time, and inviting their prayerful consideration of these requirements in the hours ahead.

Seven more votes were taken, and again, each inconclusive. The process was suspended a second time, and the senior Cardinal Priest gave the second exhortation. Ruggieri was elated.

There is no one in this chapel as capable as I am to lead the Church into the future. My votes are holding up. It's only a matter of time until a majority is formed in my favor.

As inconceivable as it was to Ruggieri and the other cardinals, after seven more votes, the results were still inconclusive. Established procedures now called for an address by the senior Cardinal Bishop, Stefano Paganelli.

No one could have anticipated the bomb shell Cardinal Paganelli was about to deliver.

CHAPTER 11

It had been eleven days since the cardinals had processed into the Sistine Chapel to begin the Conclave to elect a new pope. A long Conclave was not unprecedented. In centuries past, some had continued for months. The longest, to elect Pope Gregory X in 1572, met for almost three years.

In modern times, a Conclave for well over a week never happened. The current delay was exacting a toll on all those present. It wasn't just the length of time it was taking for a consensus to be reached – it was that no consensus was even on the horizon.

It was before a discouraged and depressed group of churchmen that Cardinal Paganelli, in his role as senior Cardinal Bishop, stood to give the address after the third suspension of voting.

He began by reiterating the stresses on the Church today, the likes of which had not been so severe in centuries.

"We have witnessed pontiff after pontiff struggle with these problems, and just when it appeared headway was being made, the same difficulties would return with a vengeance."

After so many days in this unproductive Conclave, fatigue was evident on the faces of the cardinals. Fatigue and impatience.

We've heard all this over and over – we know all this! Why is he doing this to us?

Cardinal Paganelli continued:

"We know the Holy Spirit depends on us, works through us to fulfill the Divine Plan."

Cardinal Ruggieri made the totally unacceptable breach of protocol by whispering sarcastically in the ear of the cardinal next to him:

"How nice for the senior Cardinal Bishop to grace us with a theology lecture!"

Cardinal Paganelli drove home the point that God works through humans to make a better world:

"Consider Saint John XXIII, who made the liturgy and doctrine of Catholicism more meaningful to countless millions.

"Several years later, Saint John Paul II proved to be an evangelist extraordinaire, traveling the world, visiting the faithful and promoting peace."

The impatience of the majority was palpable – almost to the boiling point – when Paganelli suddenly shifted gears in a manner that captured the attention of the total assembly, even those who were nodding off to sleep.

"Although no one, for more than six centuries, has been elected to the papacy who was not a cardinal, we are well aware that we are free to go outside this Conclave to choose the next pope.

"I want to talk to you about such a person, whom many of you know, a man of God who has earned much admiration and respect, not only from those in the religious order which he now heads, but anyone who has had the privilege to know him and work with him. I speak of the Reverend William Bracey, Superior General of the Society of Jesus."

Cardinal Paganelli went on to describe Bracey's background in dramatic detail – a Jewish immigrant to America, a convert to the faith with an outstanding record as a Jesuit. He cited his overwhelming election to be the new worldwide leader of the Society of Jesus.

"We would be hard-pressed to find another individual so qualified to lead the Church in the mid-21st century."

The senior Cardinal Bishop took his seat amidst a profound silence. The College of Cardinals sat paralyzed in total disbelief. Stefano Paganelli was suggesting a Jesuit priest, albeit an exceptional one, be the choice of the Church's senior prelates – an individual who was not even a bishop, much less a cardinal.

After a few moments, some cardinals began nodding their heads in assent – many knew this man and admired him immensely. Then a few more.

A number of the traditionalists shook their heads, clearly disapproving of Bracey's candidacy. Not only was he not a cardinal, not even a bishop, but he was a Jesuit. When they were young priests, 33 years before, another Jesuit had been pope, and he had been much too freethinking and flexible for their taste. Their memories of him were not happy ones. Cardinal Ruggieri shared these sentiments, and was tempted to rise and challenge Paganelli's suggestion vociferously.

Albert Rooney was aghast.

I know how this man has operated, both as a Provincial and as the Jesuit's Superior General. He is a liberal and a progressive. He won't get us back to the discipline of the traditional Catholic Church!

After a period of prayer, the voting continued. Following the next two votes, the smoke from the burning ballots rising above the Sistine Chapel was black, indicating to the people awaiting results in St. Peter's Square that no pope had been elected.

On the third ballot, one candidate received just over two-thirds of the votes, but it was too early for white smoke. The pealing of St. Peter's Basilica bells was yet to be heard.

CHAPTER 12

Like everyone at the Vatican and in Rome, Father William Bracey was surprised to see the Conclave was still in session.

Greater than his surprise was his sense of concern. It clearly indicated either the cardinals could not agree on who would be the best choice to lead the Church, or that none of the so-called "papabile" were willing to take on this heavy responsibility. He found both possibilities very troubling.

He changed his focus from these thoughts, and returned to preparations he was making for a meeting with visiting Jesuit provincials from South America, when his phone rang.

"Father Bracey, this is Cardinal Paganelli," said the voice from the other end.

Bracey was perplexed. "Cardinal, you couldn't be phoning unless you had left the Conclave, but I've seen no white smoke and haven't heard St. Peter's bells. What's happened?"

"I've been temporarily excused from the Conclave in order to phone you, my friend. There is a candidate who was two votes short of the required two-thirds on the last ballot, and most assuredly will be elected on the next ballot. However, this individual is not a cardinal, and we do not know whether he will accept the responsibility we are about to give him."

William Bracey was in a state of shock. There could be only one reason Cardinal Paganelli was phoning him.

"How in the name of heaven can this be?" he sputtered. "There are dozens of cardinals with the ability and the desire to assume this responsibility."

Paganelli responded, "Father, those in the Sistine Chapel cannot agree on anyone in the assembly who is capable of providing the leadership these difficult times require. Your performance over the years establishes you as someone who not only can do, but will do what is necessary to serve the people of God."

"There will be another vote shortly, and you will be the pope-elect. When that happens, will you accept?"

There was only silence from Bracey's end. Paganelli continued:

"Please come to the Apostolic Palace so you will be close to the Sistine Chapel after the vote is taken. Think this over carefully, Father Bracey. The Church has never been in greater need for strong leadership, and a man of action. You won't be doing this alone – the Holy Spirit will be at your side. A billion Catholics will be depending on you, and benefiting from your strength and guidance."

"I will leave for the Apostolic Palace right away, Your Eminence."

✳✳✳

William. Bracey had a regular driver when he left the Curia Generalizia for a meeting away from Jesuit headquarters. However, today he took a taxi, leaving inconspicuously, and alone.

As the cab ferried him through Rome to the Vatican, he reflected on what it meant to be a Jesuit. Ignatius of Loyola founded the Society of Jesus right after the start of the Protestant Reformation – a schism sparked, in great part, as a reaction to the rampant clericalism in the Catholic Church.

Part of the Constitution of the Jesuits admonishes members not to seek hierarchical rank, and to accept such authority only when absolutely necessary. But at the same time, the Jesuit motto is *Ad Majorem Dei Gloriam* – For the Greater Glory of God.

Is not my assuming the mantle of pope necessary, under these circumstances? Is this not "for the greater glory of God?"

He knew the answers to both questions had to be "yes."

He arrived at the Apostolic Palace, and was escorted to a small room, and invited to be seated.

In a few minutes, Cardinal Paganelli came in, and informed him: "The vote has been taken, and you are pope-elect. Are you ready?"

Father Bracey said "I am."

"Come with me to the Sistine Chapel," beckoned Cardinal Paganelli. "Since you are going to be the Bishop of Rome, we must now ordain you a bishop!"

CHAPTER 13

As Bracey and Paganelli entered the Sistine Chapel, the assembled cardinals broke into spontaneous applause. Father Bracey gave an awkward, self-conscious smile, feeling his current circumstances more of a fantasy than a reality. He looked toward Cardinal Paganelli with a quizzical look, as if to ask *Now what?*

The Dean of Cardinals, Federico Lanzillo, approached Bracey and shook his hand. Then he took his arm and led him to the center of the Chapel for the time-honored ceremony. He asked, "Do you accept your canonical election as Supreme Pontiff?"

Father Bracey responded: "I accept."

Lanzillo then instructed him, "Please kneel as I ordain you a bishop." As soon as his required consecration was completed, William Bracey was Pope.

White smoke poured from the chimney above the Sistine Chapel, and the sound of St. Peter's Basilica bells pealed joyfully throughout the Vatican and beyond.

The Dean then asked him, "By what name do you want to be known?"

The new Pope responded, "Francis Xavier."

His choice of names, in honor of St. Francis Xavier, was surprising to no one. Francis Xavier, one of the original followers of St. Ignatius, was the first Jesuit missionary, and devoted his life to bringing Christianity to India and other countries of eastern Asia.

Bracey admired his evangelistic zeal, his tenacity, his organizational abilities, his dedication. These were traits William Bracey emulated, and he felt a special devotion to this holy man.

Though this was a totally different "Francis" than Francis of Assisi, after whom the first Jesuit pope had named himself, some could not help wondering if his predecessor's name selection 33 years earlier hadn't also influenced William Bracey's choice.

Newly elected popes are remembered to have been in tears over the immense responsibility placed on their shoulders, and have cried as they were led to the dressing room where they would don the symbols of their new authority. Pope Francis Xavier was now taken through the aptly named Door of Tears to that dressing room, where he was fitted with his white papal cassock and zucchetto.

He was escorted to the main chair of the Chapel, was seated, and from there was greeted individually by each cardinal. Each man pledged his allegiance. The Pope in turn gave each cardinal his blessing.

From the Loggia of the Blessings balcony of St Peter's Basilica, the senior Cardinal Deacon announced to the multitude below in St. Peter's Square the centuries-old proclamation: *Annuntio vobis gaudium magnum! Habemus Papam!*

"I announce to you a great joy! We have a Pope! William Bracey. Pope Francis Xavier."

Pope Francis Xavier came forward, waved to the cheering crowd, addressed them, and gave his papal blessing, *Urbi et Orbi.* (To the City and to the World.)

***

For the former Jesuit Superior General, it had been a blur of activity from the moment the phone rang three hours earlier. He was struggling to comprehend his new role – the overwhelming responsibility that, in his wildest dreams, he could not have imagined being placed on his shoulders.

"Work as if everything depended on you, pray as if everything depended on God," Ignatius of Loyola admonished his followers.

Now, as the new Pope Francis Xavier, he was acutely conscious of the importance and wisdom of that penetrating insight.

Francis Xavier was about to face some challenges that would sorely test his mettle and his Ignatian philosophy.

CHAPTER 14

Albert Rooney checked out of the Domus Sanctae Marthae guest house, where all cardinals were required to stay during the Conclave, and returned to the Hilton Garden Inn.

He and David McLaughlin met for lunch there the next day. Since they didn't expect to find other cardinals at the hotel's Claridge Restaurant, they felt it was a good location for the private, uninterrupted chat they hoped for.

"Never in my wildest dreams did I expect to be an elector at a Conclave that would choose a mere priest, even the head of a religious order, as our next pope," McLaughlin stated, shaking his head. "We've made history!"

"I'm not particularly happy with the outcome," replied Rooney. "You've also seen him in action in the past, David. He's many steps removed from the traditions of the Church. I don't know that I'd call him a wild-eyed liberal, but that comes pretty close."

"You and I don't always see eye-to-eye on what's best for the Church right now," McLaughlin acknowledged, "but I agree William Bracey is probably too far left-of-center for these times. Elevation to pope has changed men in the past. Let's hope this may be the case with Francis Xavier.

"You know Albert, I was surprised you were asked to speak at the General Convention. How did that happen?"

"Cardinal Ruggieri nominated me. I hardly know the man."

"He knows you," McLaughlin responded with a chuckle. "Ruggieri knows everything about everybody."

"And do you know much about him?" Rooney asked.

"I was assisting with a project at the Pontifical Council for Promoting Christian Unity in 2040 when Ruggieri was appointed to his current post. I talked to several Cardinals who knew him well, and I learned a lot."

"Tell me what you know," Rooney requested.

'He's a native of southern Italy – the town of Cosenza. I understand he was an exceptionally bright student, and when he was in the seminary, his bishop sent him to Rome to study theology."

"We're about the same age" noted Rooney. "I don't recall ever seeing him at the Gregorian."

"He didn't go there" McLaughlin informed him. "He studied at the Pontifical Lateran University and was assigned as a professor at the Gregorian after a short stint as a parish priest in his home town.

"He was known for his ultra-conservative approach as a professor of moral theology – hellfire, damnation, all of that. He had a strong influence on the more traditionalist seminarians, especially those from the U.S.

"If there's nothing else Ruggieri has, it's staying power. The Roman Curia has been his professional home for many years.

"The position he holds now – as Prefect of the Congregation for the Doctrine of the Faith – he filled fifteen years before, but was removed abruptly when Pope Leo XIV was elected – a substantial shock to this ambitious man. After the election of Pope Paul VII, he got the job and the power back. Ruggieri is widely considered to be a manipulator, and very astute in achieving his goals. He always works very actively behind the scenes."

McLaughlin paused, as he considered how to sum up his insights on Ruggieri:

"There's one thing for certain, Albert. If Francis Xavier allows him to remain in this key position, he'll have his hands full!"

CHAPTER 15

Cardinal Antonio Ruggieri had a way of putting the fear of God into anyone who worked with him in any capacity. Even his physical presence and demeanor were alarming to those who challenged or disagreed with him.

Barely 5'6" tall, swarthy complexion, thick black hair with a short forehead, a solid neck and closely set dark brown eyes topped by heavy eyebrows, Ruggieri appeared to have within him the elements of an impending hurricane. When he was angry, which was often, his brow wrinkled, and his eyes pierced like glowing coals.

His somewhat ominous personal demeanor proved to be an effective adjunct to his exceptional intellect and unstinting determination. He was above all else a man accustomed to coming out on top.

As confident as he was in his own abilities, Ruggieri was troubled now. Popes had been elected before with plans to reform the Curia, and he had overtly endorsed their efforts on a consistent basis. However, with his skilled machinations and the help of his minions, he was always able to frustrate their agenda.

Now the ballgame had changed. With Francis Xavier, he anticipated problems. His sixth sense told him a storm was brewing. A new line of attack – a more creative approach – was called for to meet this challenge.

What better person with whom to brain-storm a creative approach than Dieter Kaufmann.

The day after the new pope's election, Ruggieri quietly arranged a meeting with Kaufmann, who was staying in Rome for the inauguration Mass.

"Dieter," Ruggieri greeted, him," thank you for coming over on such short notice. We are heading into rough seas, my friend, and we need a plan to navigate them without getting swamped."

Dieter Kaufmann, like everyone who dealt with Antonio Ruggieri, had a healthy respect for the Prefect's volatility, and understood his unquestionable influence on events in the Curia. At the same time, Kaufmann was a man of considerable strength, and utterly calculating in his own right. He wasn't about to be pushed around or intimidated by anyone, even Antonio Ruggieri. He could be trusted by Ruggieri to speak plainly. This, plus the fact they were of like minds regarding the necessary direction for the Church's future, made Kaufmann a trusted associate.

They retired to a sofa in Ruggieri's office, and an aide brought in a carafe of coffee and a platter of biscotti. Ruggieri got right to the point:

"This new Pope is different from his predecessors, Dieter. He's going to be a real challenge, no doubt about it. He is not a man to be manipulated – no way I can wrap him around my little finger. I'm afraid our work is cut out for us."

"Francis Xavier doesn't have the credentials," Kaufmann responded. "He wasn't a cardinal. Before his election, he wasn't even a bishop. He has no appreciation of the power structure that must be maintained."

"These Jesuits like to be recognized for their independent thinking and action," Ruggieri hissed. "They are notorious for thinking 'outside of the box' all too often.

"This troubles me greatly.

"Francis Xavier is appointing a new Secretary of State, but he's leaving the Curia intact for the time being. I am still worried, though. More than past pontiffs, this man will surely insinuate himself into Curia matters and the way the Church hierarchy operates. I think it won't be long before this happens."

"Antonio," Kaufmann stressed, "derailing his train before it gains speed has to be our highest priority. The work must start now. You need to bring together those men who think like us – you know who they are – men with influence, whom we can count on, and it has to be as soon as possible."

Then and there, Antonio Ruggieri decided to contact like-minded churchmen before the papal inauguration to make sure they remained in Rome afterwards for this very crucial meeting.

"Success is a function of thinking ahead," Cardinal Ruggieri told Kaufmann. "You need to outflank your adversary before he outflanks you!"

CHAPTER 16

The speed of events for Pope Francis Xavier appeared out of control.

His move into the papal apartments, introductions to all the employees of the Apostolic Palace, and meetings with the Camerlengo and other officials to fill him in on important pending issues occurred at a dizzying pace. Moreover, he still had to prepare his homily for the Inaugural Mass, and tie up loose ends from his former assignment as Jesuit Superior General. The pace was both exhilarating and exhausting, and left him little time to absorb the momentous chain of events that had thrust him into the most important position in all of Christendom.

The Inaugural Mass followed his election by four days. Held outside the doors of St. Peter's Basilica, the same setting as the funeral Mass for Paul VII, tens of thousands crowded St. Peter's Square. With religious and political leaders from around the world in the chairs on each side of the altar, Francis Xavier spoke to themes that, during the 21st century, most popes had addressed at their inauguration.

In his homily, the new pope called for world peace and for the protection of the environment. He expressed concern over the continual secularization of the Earth's cultures, and beseeched world leaders to let moral and ethical principles inform the decisions they make that impact the sanctity and quality of life.

It was a well-stated and uplifting homily, interrupted frequently by applause with unrestrained cheering at its conclusion, all indicating his message was well-received.

Much of great importance, however, was left unsaid. The Pope had already begun to formulate his priorities and spell them out in an Apostolic Letter he was drafting.

Had he revealed his full agenda in the homily, it would have shocked almost everyone – both those present in St. Peter's Square and the TV audience around the world – and would have spawned a substantial wave of anxiety among the Catholic Church hierarchy.

CHAPTER 17

Nestled in the hills northeast of Rome lies the Villa San Giuseppe, a beautiful estate dating back to the 18th century, now owned by the prominent Ponticello family of Florence. They often made the site available to members of the Church hierarchy who needed a private meeting place, far removed from the prying eyes of the media.

This was an ideal venue for his planning meeting, and Ruggieri invited eight cardinals to attend: three officials of the Curia, and five cardinal archbishops who shared his conviction that a lack of discipline threatened to irreparably damage the foundations of the Church.

Albert Rooney was on the invitation list. Ruggieri had been quite impressed with him at the General Congregation, They shared a world view, nurtured the same priorities, and suffered the same anxiety about the weakness and free-thinking liberalism now rife among the laity.

Cardinal Ruggieri was planning the agenda for this meeting, to be held just three days after the papal inauguration, when Father Gustavo Bivona, who served as his secretary, brought him a letter that had just arrived from the Vatican.

It was an Apostolic Letter from Pope Francis Xavier, addressed to all the bishops of the universal Church. It was written in Latin, its title being *Ad Ecclesiae Renovationem* (For the Renewal of the Church), but was accompanied by an Italian and an English translation, given many churchmen no longer understood Latin. Ruggieri pondered, as he perused its contents:

His Holiness is moving faster than I expected.

In the initial pages there were no big surprises – the need to update the administrative structure of the Church, the paucity of priestly vocations, the need to address forthrightly the clerical sex abuse scandals that wouldn't go away, and the persistent undermining of the family in western society.

Finally, His Holiness addressed the continual dwindling numbers of the faithful, and among those who still called themselves Catholic, the weak participation in the Church.

"We have been concerned about this trend for many decades, and have tried several solutions to reverse it, but to little avail.

"The one thing we are not doing is finding out what the people of God really think. What is keeping them away from church? What are their real problems? What are their unrealized expectations? We truly do not know this.

"Earlier this century, we asked the Church's bishops to obtain this information and advise us of the results. This effort was not particularly successful."

Ruggieri's eyes bulged and his jaw dropped as he read on.

"To address this problem, we intend to elevate a number of laymen – from all over the world – to the level of cardinal."

Anxiety swelled in the Cardinal's chest. The paper quivered in his trembling hand as he continued.

"We will ask them to ascertain the needs, difficulties and aspirations of the laity in their communities, and bring this information for discussion at the highest Church levels, so adequate solutions, rising from the real needs, concerns and aspirations of our laity, can be devised and implemented."

Ruggieri was dumbfounded! He reread this section in Latin, then Italian and finally in English to make sure it said what he thought it said. Then he gasped.

This is totally and utterly preposterous! What the Pope is proposing would wreck havoc on the entire hierarchical structure of the Church!

Antonio Ruggieri slammed a fist on his desk.

God's plan is not a democracy, where the faithful vote for what they want! It is the Church's role, and the sacred obligation of the hierarchy, to guide the faithful on the path to Heaven. This Pope threatens to destroy a foundation carefully created over the millennia!

Ruggieri now knew what the most crucial item on the agenda for the meeting at Villa San Giuseppe had to be.

CHAPTER 18

Albert Rooney rented a car with a driver for his trip to Villa San Giuseppe. He left mid-afternoon for the journey that, with commuter traffic, would take over an hour.

It was pleasantly warm, the fields a radiant green, and the trees that lined the road casting long shadows across the landscape. Leaving Rome behind with its crowded and bustling urban environment was a welcome respite for the Cardinal.

The responsibilities, activities and pressures of the General Congregation and Conclave had taken a toll, and he was exhausted. He was hopeful this meeting would offer a refreshing change of venue, and a less demanding agenda. He was to be sorely disappointed in his expectations.

The car climbed up a hill on a winding road through an olive orchard, and then past old vineyards with row after row of vines laden with copious bunches of luscious grapes, ripe for the harvest, to the Villa San Giuseppe, a 300 year-old stone structure with mottled yellow walls and a red clay tile roof. The view of the valley below was gorgeous.

On his arrival, Cardinal Ruggieri introduced Rooney to the others, who had already arrived: Cardinals Flavio Scarpelli, Prefect of the Congregation for Divine Worship and the Discipline of the Sacraments; Francois Basse, Prefect of the Congregation for the Evangelization of Peoples; Angelo Molinaro, Prefect of the Congregation for Bishops; Dieter Kaufmann, Archbishop of Munich; Vittorio Tornebene, Archbishop of Milan; Antonin Zoromski, Archbishop of Krakow; and Umberto Sciara, Archbishop of Naples.

Cardinal Rooney felt he had just been introduced to a "who's who" of the Church's movers and shakers. He had heard of all of them, and was aware of the key role each played in their respective spheres of influence. He had already met Cardinals Zoromski, Scarpelli and Basse at the General Congregation, and knew them to be conservative thinkers just as he and Ruggieri were.

He was aware of an important fringe benefit of his being included in this meeting.

Appointments to the Curia are made by the Pope, but the advice of other Church leaders plays a significant role in his selections.

When they sat down to dinner in a private dining room at the Villa, the conversation was casual and congenial. After desert and coffee, cordials were served, and Cardinal Ruggieri got right to the business at hand.

"We at this table have a responsibility to see to it that, when the Church veers from her time-proven disciplines and practices, we do what we must to correct her course."

Heads nodded around the table.

He reminded his colleagues of actions those present had taken in the past to modify or reverse papal directions they considered ill-advised.

Cardinal Rooney found himself a little anxious at the tenor of Ruggieri's remarks. He spoke up:

"I agree the change of direction wrought by Vatican II was most undesirable – that can't be argued. But doesn't there come a point, after the Pope has made his decision, that it is our responsibility to carry it out?"

The other cardinals around the table gave Rooney a condescending smile.

"You are new to our group, and our philosophy, Cardinal Rooney," responded Ruggieri. "Let me explain it this way.

"St Peter himself was a flawed man. We know that. Jesus had to correct him a number of times, sometimes even scold him. However, even though he was fallible, Jesus chose him to be the 'rock' upon which He would build His Church.

"After the Ascension, Peter continued to make mistakes, and the apostles had to set him straight. That was their role. It was their duty.

"The Pope is the successor to St. Peter, and we are the successors to the apostles. If the Pope makes decisions that are inadvisable, we must do what we can to see that he puts the Church back on its proper course."

Ruggieri now turned his attention to the Apostolic Letter they all had received from Francis Xavier. He gave some attention to the curial reforms to which the Pope had alluded, how ill-advised they were, and reiterated that he and his colleagues had prevented them in the past and would obstruct their implementation again this time.

Finally he addressed the Pope's "outrageous" plan to appoint lay cardinals – the main topic of the evening.

"It is incredible, unconscionable and shocking that Francis Xavier has the audacity to even think about creating a group of lay cardinals to represent the attitudes of the laity. This violates God's plan for humanity, and threatens the historic foundations upon which the Church is built."

Ruggieri left no stone unturned as he enumerated the reasons why this was an extremely dangerous idea.

"This will not only give a pulpit to every malcontent in Christendom, but threatens to undermine the very authority and organization of those who lead the Church," he asserted with emphasis.

He reached into his briefcase.

"I have drafted a letter to His Holiness, expressing our concern about his intention to appoint lay cardinals. You will see that despite our real feelings of outrage, I stated this very diplomatically.

"I have requested a meeting with him to explore this subject further. I am asking all of you here tonight to join me in signing this expression of concern, and our request for a meeting."

Everyone nodded their assent. All stepped forward to sign.

On the drive back to Rome, Rooney ruminated about the extraordinary few days he had spent in Rome, and especially the tenor of this evening's gathering. He felt uncomfortable with the Machiavellian approach these Church leaders were taking in their dealings with the Pope.

It didn't fit with his vision of how the Church's most influential prelates did – or should – relate to the Supreme Pontiff. On the other hand, he firmly believed that, since Vatican II, the Church had lost its way, and the mid-20th century Vatican Council was the source of most of its problems.

Perhaps – just perhaps – my participation in Cardinal Ruggieri's inner circle would contribute to correcting the errors of the past 80 years. If that's the case, I would, indeed, be doing God's work.

I must think this over.

As the car wended its way back down the dark roads to Rome, Albert Rooney could never have foreseen how tonight's conspiracy would unleash a chain of events that would change his life in ways beyond his imagining.

CHAPTER 19

The Apostolic Letter of Pope Francis Xavier set off a worldwide media feeding frenzy. TV anchors descended on the Vatican, reporters interrogated anyone who would stand still long enough to be interviewed.

"What is behind this decision to appoint lay cardinals?"

"What will this do to the College of Cardinals?"

"Does this represent a strategy by the new Pope to remove the traditional authority from the bishops?"

The questions were endless.

The phones rang incessantly at the Vatican Press Office as the print, broadcast and electronic media looked for answers to questions no one was prepared to answer.

Bishops throughout the world were besieged by members of the Fourth Estate.

"How will you be affected by this change?"

"What will it mean now to be a bishop?"

"What is this Pope thinking?"

Official diocesan newspapers relegated the story to back pages, and their editorials were far from enthusiastic. Even the independent Catholic press, typically much more sanguine about progressive change, expressed utter amazement.

News of the letter had an immediate impact in the life of local parishes. Conservative parishioners were appalled by the prospect of a lay cardinal.

The Church knows what is best for the faithful. Why would the Holy See establish a mechanism for disgruntled Catholics to sound off and vent their spleen?

Catholics of a more liberal and progressive frame of mind were elated by the news.

It's about time! No one ever seems to care about our reactions to directives from Rome. Now we just might have a voice!

A similar conservative-progressive dichotomy existed among the clergy, among priests in particular. Most bishops and cardinals, however, did not favor such a change. Although some believed the established Church structure was God-given, many feared their authority might be diminished by this innovation. They were naturally hesitant to voice opinions contrary to the Pope, but at the same time, avoided endorsing the initiative.

As the weeks went by, and nothing further was heard from the Holy See about the Pope's plans, media interest waned. For individual Catholics as well, the issue moved to the back burner, although some still wondered what would be the Pope's next steps.

Many of the hierarchy were of the opinion that nothing significant would happen. They believed Pope Francis Xavier was just flexing his muscles, making clear who was in charge, and that was that.

Nothing could have been further from the truth.

***

The reactions to his Apostolic Letter were very disturbing to Francis Xavier. He feared he may have acted precipitously.

Bishops throughout the world expressed concern such an action would damage the Church – a Church whose membership was already dwindling. Prelates across the globe did not hesitate to make their reservations known to Rome. One bishop even had the temerity to write the Pontiff critically about the plan:

"It will add a significant note of uncertainty to those who are struggling to meet the demands of their faith, and will anger and even scandalize the large number of the faithful who religiously follow the Church's dictates without questioning them."

Many traditional Catholics were already disgusted by so-called "cafeteria Catholics" who insisted on picking and choosing what Church practices they were going to follow. A papal initiative giving them a voice would only make things worse.

The letter the Pope received from Cardinal Ruggieri, signed by his like-minded associates, was of special concern. Ruggieri had a reputation for getting his way, or when he couldn't, proving himself to be a spoiler. Francis Xavier took Ruggieri's letter very seriously.

High on the Pope's agenda was the appointment of a new Secretary of State, someone who would be his close advisor and also know how to deal with the Curia. Because of the brouhaha over his Apostolic Letter, this appointment took on an added note of urgency.

Most opinions expressed by the media and Vatican insiders assumed the Pope would appoint a European in order to draw attention to his strong interest in revitalizing the historic roots of the Church.

That is not what Francis Xavier had in mind.

CHAPTER 20

Cardinal Sanjay Patel and Father William Bracey's friendship went back several years, long before Bracey became Superior General of the Jesuits.

From his first priestly ministry at a small church in his native India, Patel proved to be a competent diplomat. Within his community, there was a great deal of tension between the Hindus and the Muslims, as well as between them and the minority Catholic population. He was able to diffuse a number of potentially explosive situations, helping groups with little common ground learn how to live together in peace as neighbors.

As his diplomatic abilities were recognized by his archbishop, and acknowledged by Rome, he was sent to the Sorbonne for advanced studies in law and political science. Afterwards, he received further training in papal diplomacy at the Pontifical Ecclesiastical Academy.

Patel was then assigned to the Holy See's Secretariat of State. He filled several diplomatic posts, and was ordained a bishop. His last post was Papal Nuncio (ambassador) to Canada.

In 2037, Father Bracey was introduced to Bishop Patel when he attended a conference of North American Jesuit provincials in Ottawa. The two formed an immediate bond. Over the years, they corresponded frequently about issues of mutual interest, and got together whenever possible.

Patel was elected Archbishop of Bombay in 2040, and shortly thereafter, elevated to Cardinal. As Jesuit Superior General, whenever William Bracey visited the Jesuit provinces in India, and his travels brought him to Mumbai, he made it a point to see his good friend Sanjay.

After the Inauguration Mass, Patel spent several days in Rome to do some work for the Pontifical Council for Legislative Texts. He was making preparations to return to Mumbai, when his phone rang. He responded to a familiar voice on the other end:

"What an unexpected and pleasant surprise, Your Holiness! I was just about to return to India."

Without chatting or engaging in any pleasantries, the Pope interjected, "Sanjay, can you delay your return? It is very important that I see you as soon as possible."

Patel replied, "I'll be over right away."

***

When Patel arrived at the papal apartments, the two engaged in some casual small talk. Francis Xavier wanted to catch up on what had been happening with Sanjay. Since their last visit, it was pretty obvious what had been going on with William Bracey.

Then His Holiness got to the point:

"Sanjay, I need you to be my Secretary of State, and I need you badly."

He reiterated the challenges he faced. They seemed to be growing by the day.

"I haven't replaced any prefects or other Curia officials. I frankly don't know the personnel that well – who should go, who should stay.

"I am viewed as a complete outsider. I fear disturbing the Curia status quo at this time will likely do more harm than good. In the long run, I hope to make major curial reforms and changes, but I feel certain rocking the boat now is inadvisable.

"You are in a unique position to help me. You know the administration well, but you are not part of the 'cartel.' As you know, there is a clique that is as thick as thieves, but you, thank God, are not a card-carrying member of that crowd.

"I trust you implicitly, and want you to run interference for me. I need you to be my right-hand man. I am sorry to put this burden on you, but I know of no man this side of heaven who could be more helpful to me."

"I am honored to serve you, Your Holiness. You can count on me."

"I knew I could, old friend.

"I have another request. When you and I are working together with no one else with us, please call me by my Christian name. I truly think it would help create the right atmosphere for our problem-solving efforts."

"I agree with you, William, and I will do so."

CHAPTER 21

After reviewing with his new Secretary of State the many concerns he had, including those in his Apostolic Letter, he handed Patel a copy of the letter he had received from Cardinal Ruggieri and his faction:

"Sanjay, read this."

Patel read it carefully, put it down, and sat for a minute or two, looking out the window.

"William, may I speak frankly?"

"Of course you can," the Pope replied.

"I think your Apostolic Letter was premature. You were brand new to your office, and you immediately fired off a broadside at the present structure. It ignited a firestorm."

Patel reread the letter, shaking his head.

"I am especially worried about Ruggieri's reaction. He is powerful and influential at the Curia, and doesn't like to be crossed. He can be very vindictive."

Francis Xavier sat back in his chair, his fingers steepled in front of his face.

"You're right. My letter was done too impulsively. I never expected such strong reaction to it from every corner of the globe. I just wanted to make it clear, from the start, this Pope has no intention of settling for things as they are."

While Patel ruminated, considering what he would say next, the Pope's mind flashed back to another time – years ago – when he had also acted precipitously.

When he was President of Santa Clara University in California and ordered the disbanding of an ultra-conservative student organization he didn't think represented the academic principles of the University, he reprimanded the faculty member who served as the group's advisor.

Students held protests outside his office and the faculty threatened a vote of "no confidence" because they felt he was violating academic freedom. Since then, he had tried hard – usually with success – to carefully consider the unintended consequences of his actions and avoid similar mistakes

Obviously, I failed again this time. I thought I had learned my lesson.

Francis Xavier came back to the present moment as Sanjay addressed him again:

"There's a story I must tell you" he said at last, "though I feel some reluctance in doing so. Do you remember Cardinal Christian Bauer?"

"He was murdered several years ago," the Pope recalled. " I believe it was the year before I was elected Superior General. That would have been 2040."

"That's correct," Patel responded. "Do you remember the circumstances surrounding his death?"

"I'm afraid not."

"It was shortly after Paul VII's election. Bauer had been Prefect of the Congregation for the Doctrine of the Faith, and had been appointed to this position after Pope Leo XIV removed Cardinal Ruggieri from this assignment and offered him a position of lesser responsibility. No one knows the reason for this change.

"Since his demotion, Ruggieri made it clear he would do whatever it took to be reappointed to his former position of power.

"After Pope Leo XIV died, all curial administrators offered pro forma resignations. However, as was expected, his successor Pope Paul VII reappointed most of them – with one dramatic exception. The new pope made it clear that he was undecided whether to reappoint Bauer, or to bring back Ruggieri as Prefect of the Congregation for the Doctrine of the Faith. He set a deadline for making his decision."

Patel paused as if reconstructing the story in his own mind, rubbed a hand across his forehead, then continued.

"Two days prior to Paul VII's deadline, Cardinal Bauer was found dead in his spacious study by his housekeeper. He had been shot in the heart. The circumstances surrounding this tragedy were strange indeed.

"First of all, he was seated on a sofa at the far end of his study. The sofa faced the door to the study, which was open and which led to the apartment's foyer and entrance. In his lap was a book, on his face, reading glasses. He kept the door of his apartment locked. Had someone knocked, he would have naturally put the book aside and removed the reading glasses as he went to let his guest in.

"Even if someone with a key had entered, he would have surely risen to his feet. There was no forced entry. No matter what circumstances gave the perpetrator entry, Cardinal Bauer did not move or put his book down. Very strange.

"Powder marks prove whoever fired the shot did so at close range. Surprisingly, very little blood flowed from his wound."

The Pope interrupted Patel, "What do the Carabinieri attribute that to?"

"The forensic pathologist said it's possible to fire into the heart and have it stop beating immediately, while, at the same time, not hitting any major blood vessels. That's a very rare occurrence, since it's almost impossible to do intentionally."

The Pope asked, "Was it a robbery – were valuables missing?"

"No valuables of any kind. Not even his wallet or wrist watch. No other belongings. But files were removed from his desk. Someone was looking for something, scattering paper all over the floor."

"Was there an autopsy?" the Pope asked.

"The Carabinieri did not order an autopsy. They said it was obvious he died from the gunshot wound. There was some speculation however, that the gunshot wound was not the cause of death. It is believed by some that someone shot a dead man.

"Since Bauer had no living family, the Church authorities in his home Archdiocese of Munich could have asked for an autopsy. It was suggested to them they do so, but the Archbishop of Munich specifically requested there be no autopsy – said he felt it would desecrate the body. I have never heard of an autopsy being considered a desecration, but that's the reason the Archbishop gave."

Francis Xavier thought for a moment.

"Was the Archbishop, by any chance, Dieter Kaufmann, one of the cardinal's who signed Ruggieri's letter?"

"Yes, it was," Patel replied and then continued:

"But William, I am in no way inferring Ruggieri had anything to do with this murder. God forbid! And there is not one iota of evidence tying him to this terrible deed.

"Ruggieri's detractors whispered about the possibility. He made it abundantly clear to anyone who would listen that he was determined to get the assignment as Prefect back by whatever means necessary. I think it is important for you to know the circumstances, and what some people were saying."

***

The Pope leaned back in his chair, locked his hands behind his head, and took a few slow, deep breaths.

"Getting back to the letter from Ruggieri and his 'Gang of Eight,' what do you think my response should be?"

"First of all, you should not answer the letter immediately. A fast response could indicate weakness. You should wait a few weeks, and let this squall blow over. Time will take off some of the heat and make reasonable discussion more possible. At that point, you should set up the meeting the group requested.

"They will push you to reverse the initiative you announced. Perhaps they will press hard. If you cave on any key issue you will relinquish your position of leadership. You can't do that. But you should be ready to make some kind of compromise, so they believe they have come away with something."

Francis Xavier smiled. Patel's years at the Pontifical Ecclesiastical Academy and as a Vatican diplomat were proving themselves to be time well-spent, and his own choice of Secretary of State well-made.

"Ever since I realized my timing was off, I've been thinking about that, Sanjay. And I think I have figured out the compromise to offer."

CHAPTER 22

Antonio Ruggieri was lost in thought as he crossed St. Peter's Square on his way to the Apostolic Palace this late autumn morning. The temperature was a robust 45° F., but an arriving cold front brought with it a strong north wind that bit unremittingly at all who were exposed. It was unusually raw for the last week in November, but Ruggieri was oblivious to the penetrating chill.

Much was at stake at this meeting. Two months had passed since he and eight other cardinals requested a meeting with Pope Francis Xavier to discuss his intention to appoint lay cardinals. His Holiness finally responded to their request two weeks ago, when he invited them to come and see him late this morning.

As he walked, Ruggieri was focused on what it would take to make this meeting go his way.

Our new Pope doesn't have the experience, or the insider contacts he needs to drive his agenda forward. I don't care how good he was at leading the Jesuits. He's going to get a run for his money if he tries the same approach with the Holy See. He won't get any cooperation from the Curia – guaranteed!

The evening before, he had summoned his eight colleagues to a planning session at his residence.

"We can't lose sight of how important it is to convince His Holiness it would be the height of folly for him to carry out the ill-conceived escapade he contemplates," the Cardinal emphasized forcefully.

He told the others he would assume the role of spokesman for the group and outlined the incisive arguments he planned to make.

Cardinal Kaufmann interjected, addressing his remarks to the other seven, with Ruggieri nodding in approval:

"Should His Holiness have questions for any of us, it is essential we stay 'on message.' In no way can we deviate from the plan as outlined by Cardinal Ruggieri. We must not compromise our objective, even by one iota."

None in the group expressed any disagreement.

Three minutes after Cardinal Ruggieri entered the Apostolic Palace, Cardinal Rooney crossed St. Peter's Square alone. The chilly weather exacerbated his troubled state of mind.

Antonio Ruggieri is right, of course. His Holiness' intention to water down the College of Cardinals by opening the door to laymen is an extremely bad idea. On the other hand, the Pope is the Pope. By what right does a man decide when to obey, and when not? Is that not at the very heart of the problems the Church faces today? Where is the line drawn between disagreement and disobedience?

When all nine cardinals had arrived at the Apostolic Palace, they were taken to the Pope's private library. Several minutes later, Francis Xavier entered the room with his Secretary of State, Sanjay Patel.

***

Francis Xavier greeted them warmly, shaking each man's hand in turn, and invited them to be seated at the conference table.

He began by reviewing the critical problems the Church was facing, and had been facing for decades – problems regarding which he knew they all agreed:

- *the church pews are almost empty;*

- *many of the faithful ignore directives coming from the hierarchy;*

- *western society was becoming dangerously secularized;*

- *and finally, the number of people who call themselves Catholic is dwindling.*

"How we communicate with the faithful," His Holiness went on, "or – more to the point – how we have failed to communicate, seems to me to be the key issue confronting us. Church leaders and the faithful have been talking _over_ each other, or _at_ each other, but not _to_ each other."

Francis Xavier stood and paced back and forth behind the table, his arms folded, before he continued.

"In an age where democracy and individualism is playing an increasingly important role, in a new age of liberation in many parts of the world, Catholics do not feel they have any influence on Church issues that affect them. No one hears them and if they do, no one is interested in what they are saying."

As Francis Xavier spoke, Ruggieri's face was flushed with anger.

Doesn't this man know it never has made–and never will make– any difference what the people think? Their moral duty is to follow the dictates of Church leadership, and not question them!

The Pope then stated:

"The people need representatives in the Church to whom they can speak freely, who not only hear them, but will see their concerns are taken seriously at the highest levels, and proper solutions are devised and implemented."

As he finished, Francis Xavier returned to his chair at the head of the table and sat down. "Cardinal Ruggieri, I am anxious to hear your views."

Antonio Ruggieri had prepared a carefully-worded, well-polished dissertation. Wearing a supercilious smirk on his face, he stood before the Pope and the other cardinals like a courtroom lawyer, about to destroy the case of his opponent.

Ruggieri reviewed how the key Church traditions had developed over the centuries, and how they helped countless people achieve holiness. He emphasized:

"It is essential the faithful follow the precepts laid down by the Holy See, and communicated and enforced by the bishops and the priests – precepts that have stood the test of time."

Francis Xavier paid close attention to Ruggieri's words, and especially his body language.

I think there is a hidden agenda in his pious statements. He talks about the mission of the Church, but my gut tells me his chief concern is the power of the hierarchy.

Ruggieri, coming into his stride, launched into an argument he had not shared with his colleagues the evening before. It sounded more like a threat than a point of view:

"You know, Your Holiness, the Church has undergone two devastating schisms – first with eastern Christianity in the 11th century, and then the Protestant Reformation in the 16th.

"Now dioceses throughout the world have become grievously divided by the Apostolic Letter you issued in September. It is polarizing the laity, and driving priest against priest, bishop against bishop. This proposal of yours may well lead to a latter-day schism."

Ruggieri stood at the edge of the conference table, planted the palms of his hands firmly on it, and leaned toward Francis Xavier. He offered the Pope a condescending smile.

"Should that happen, Your Holiness, history would rate your papacy as a tragic chapter in the life of the Church."

Ruggieri returned to his seat.

As he finished his tirade, seven of the cardinals present – Scarpelli, Basse, Molinaro, Kaufmann, Tornebenne, Zoromski and Sciara – nodded in agreement. Albert Rooney stared straight ahead, expressionless, but he was churning inside.

Ruggieri's threat of possible schism is a virtual challenge – an insult to the Holy Father! This is a clear overstatement, most likely a ploy to intimidate the Pope. Rank insubordination!

A number of seconds passed while everyone in the room remained silent. Finally, Cardinal Rooney felt compelled to say something to ameliorate the confrontational tone of Ruggieri's presentation. The politician in Albert Rooney rose to the fore:

"Your Holiness, to ensure that such an unfortunate outcome not come to fruition, perhaps it might be wise to devise a way to test the potential effectiveness of the program you propose to launch. You can conduct an experiment, limited in scope, before you embark on so significant a change in Church governance. That way, you'll have a better idea of any results – either worthwhile or undesirable – that might occur."

Such a course of action, Rooney calculated, would delay the Pope's initiative indefinitely, and most likely kill it.

Ruggieri was dumbfounded – and horrified! This was not part of the game plan!

How dare Rooney come up with an approach the group had not discussed, and I have not endorsed!

Ruggieri was not looking for any such compromise. He was used to getting his way, even with popes. He wanted Francis Xavier to put this plan aside – permanently!

A Mona Lisa-like smile became visible on the Pope's lips. Rooney's suggestion was the answer to a prayer.

Chapter 23

"Cardinal Rooney is exhibiting the good judgment he's so well-known for. I agree we need to test the potential effectiveness of my plan, and I believe I know the way."

Cardinal Ruggieri was flabbergasted. It was clear he had lost the initiative and that one of his own – Rooney, a signatory to the letter that resulted in this meeting – had betrayed him. Angry and frustrated, he decided, though, he couldn't go after Rooney in front of the Pope without appearing weak and doing more damage than had already been done.

The Pope announced his intention:

"Rather than elevating a number of laymen throughout the world to cardinals, I will appoint just one – a test case – with a clear mandate as to what he should do and the time frame for accomplishing it. This will give us a fix – on a very small scale – to determine its effectiveness in receiving feedback from the laity before creating the position as a permanent part of the Church's administration."

Rooney felt a surge of apprehension. The realization he had made a strategic mistake was beginning to overwhelm him.

Ruggieri and the other seven cardinals are glaring at me. No wonder! I shouldn't have said anything. Why didn't I keep my mouth shut?

"Since this is to be a pilot program," Francis Xavier continued, "our lay cardinal will hold this position only as long as I am Pope, or until we expand the initiative to be a new and permanent Order of the College of Cardinals."

The level of anxiety Ruggieri and his "Gang of Eight" were experiencing pervaded the room and was evident to the Pope and to Cardinal Patel. They stared at Francis Xavier blankly, like deer caught in a car's headlights.

"The experiment should be conducted in Europe or the United States," the Pope explained further, "where secularism is most rampant. However, I don't think Europe is the best choice, since European Catholics tend to be too blasé about what the Church does and, too often, they don't seem to even care. Americans, on the other hand, are more concerned and much more willing to be vocal about the role of the laity in the Church.

"From my point-of-view, America is the best choice. And I think Chicago would be the perfect city, since it's in the Midwest and doesn't represent the extremes of the country, geographically or in attitudes. Chicago seems to many to be the most American of cities."

The Pope turned to Cardinal Rooney.

"Albert, that is your Archdiocese, and I am asking you to take on this assignment. You have a sterling reputation as a chairman of committees for the U.S. Conference of Catholic Bishops. I can think of no one more capable of running this experiment successfully."

Rooney's heart sank.

"I want you to nominate someone who has broad experience in life, and by necessity should be at least middle-age. Not a Church employee and not necessarily a large donor. Someone who has been active in his parish, is well thought of, is not considered an ideologue, is intelligent, articulate, a good listener and dedicated.

"This lay cardinal will clearly need your support in this assignment, both personal and staff-wise. Any out-of-pocket expenses will be taken care of by the Holy See."

Albert Rooney could not conceive that this calamity was actually happening to him.

Happening to me? No, I brought this disaster on myself! A few ill-conceived words, and I may have damaged my career irreparably!

"Once you have identified the right man, submit his name to me, the details of his background and your proposed plan of action. After I've approved, we will arrange for his elevation to cardinal."

A wave of regret washed over Cardinal Rooney. The ball was in his court now, and he had no way of knowing what the outcome would be. He was certain, though, his life would never be the same again.

"I want all of you here to keep the contents of this meeting completely confidential" the Pope admonished them. "I will announce the experiment at the appropriate time."

Cardinal Ruggieri fumed!

This so-called "experiment" will be the media event of the decade. It will create unrealistic expectations among the laity. Once Pandora's Box is opened, it will be extremely difficult to close it!

CHAPTER 24

As his flight for home took off from da Vinci Airport, Cardinal Rooney was trying to sort out the events since the death of Pope Paul VII: the funeral, the General Congregation, the Conclave with the extraordinary election of a Jesuit priest, the meeting at Villa San Giuseppe, the session Ruggieri's faction had with the Pope, and his inappropriate comments leading to the unwelcome assignment the Holy Father had given him

Primarily on his mind, and troubling him, was a meeting with Ruggieri right after the session with Francis Xavier. He expected Cardinal Ruggieri to be furious with him for going off script, but to his surprise, Ruggieri greeted him warmly when he entered his office.

"A minor set-back," Ruggieri asserted. "These things happen. He was probably planning to introduce a compromise anyway.

"I am actually quite pleased that you are the one responsible for this so-called experiment, Cardinal Rooney. I expect you to see to it that it does not prove to be successful. I look forward to hearing how you are going to prevent it from getting traction."

Rooney was torn.

He had no desire to see the Pope create an Order of lay cardinals. He believed it would strengthen the current progressive trends in the Church, compounding the damage already done by Vatican II.

However, he was firmly convinced the authority of the Pope was God-given, that the Holy Father was the Vicar of Christ, and through him the Holy Spirit guides humanity in its quest for the Kingdom of Heaven.

There must be a reason God moved the cardinals to choose this particular man to occupy the Chair of Peter.

In spite of his faux pas at the meeting with the Pope, Albert Rooney still saw himself ascending to a position of greater authority in the Church by becoming the head of one of the curial commissions. If he alienated Ruggieri or any other senior curial officials, he knew they wouldn't give him favorable recommendations and could effectively hurt his career.

But if he alienated the Pope – the man who made all curial appointments – he would have absolutely no chance for advancement.

For now, the only reasonable course for me is to implement this assignment, and do it well. I really don't have to sabotage a plan that will eventually self-destruct.

He mulled over his rationale.

The folly of this whole initiative is bound to become apparent to the Pope. When the results are in, he'll understand why he should not launch the full program. The vast majority of cardinals will unite to drive this decision home to him.

As his plane soared homeward over the Atlantic Ocean, Albert Rooney put his seat in the reclining position, relaxing at last, feeling confident he knew what to do and that he was on the right track .

CHAPTER 25

Father Dan Sullivan was engaged in his usual Wednesday morning ritual – seated at his desk and writing the homily he planned to give for the two Sunday Masses at which he would preside. But he found it difficult to concentrate on the task at hand.

Two weeks ago, he met with his Archbishop, Cardinal Rooney, to make his case for a second six-year assignment as Pastor of Old St. Patrick's Church.

Pastors at Old St. Pat's were routinely given second terms. This was a unique church in many ways, and it took more than an average parish priest to provide the leadership required. Second terms weren't the exception – they were the rule. Sometimes even a third. There appeared to be no reason why Father Sullivan wouldn't stay on.

Why, then, had Cardinal Rooney asked him to meet with him again?

Something must be wrong. I have no idea what it could be.

Old St. Pat's was not only unique for Chicago – in many ways, it was unique for the nation.

Constructed in 1856, it was the oldest public building to survive the Great Fire of 1871. This historical fact, along with its architecture and Thomas O'Shaughnessy's beautiful artwork – stunning stencils of Celtic-inspired images on the walls and ceiling and stained glass windows depicting Irish saints – put Old St. Pat's on the list of the National Register of Historic Places.

Unfortunately, as the years passed and as the original members of the congregation moved on, the area around the church became an unsavory skid row. By the mid-20th century, only a handful of people were on hand for Mass on Sundays.

Because of its historical significance, the structure could not be torn down. In 1983, Cardinal Joseph Bernadin, the Archbishop of Chicago, looked for a priest willing to take on the task of reviving this house of worship, and Father Jack Wall stepped up to the plate.

Father Wall met this challenge head-on.

He made it his mission to appeal to Catholics, especially young adults, who were disaffected, or had left the Church entirely, by emphasizing Old St. Pat's was there to serve them, rather than they being there to serve the institution, an attitude all too common in many parishes.

His philosophy of creating a vibrant church took off, and people who lived dozens of miles away flocked to Old St. Pat's on Sundays. There was an excitement and vitality to this exceptional community, evidenced by a dynamic liturgy, an atmosphere of welcome and acceptance, successful local, national and international outreach programs, and the building of a parochial school – a first for Chicago in many years.

Eventually, gentrification reached the area and Old St. Pat's became the center of a lively residential neighborhood.

Father Sullivan arrived at the Cardinal's Lincoln Park mansion at the appointed time and was ushered into the study. Rooney, seated at his desk, did not look up or acknowledge Sullivan's presence. Now Dan Sullivan was certain something was wrong.

***

Finally, the Cardinal lifted his eyes to meet Sullivan's.

"Sit down, Dan," he said, gesturing to a chair opposite his desk. He rose and walked around the desk and leaned back against its front with his arms crossed.

"Can I totally trust you to keep a very serious matter in strict confidence?"

"Of course, Your Eminence," Father Sullivan replied, with a sense of relief. Whatever the issue, it became clear to him it didn't involve his request for a second six-year term.

"You are familiar with the Apostolic Letter the Holy Father sent last autumn, where he talked about appointing lay cardinals."

"Of course."

"He is taking an extraordinary step, Dan – a truly extraordinary step – and it looks like it is going to involve someone in your parish."

Rooney went on to describe the recent meeting in Rome, the limited trial the Pope decided on, and the responsibility Cardinal Rooney was given for implementing it.

"I thought about looking for candidates at several of our parishes, but felt in most cases I'd be looking for a needle in a haystack, not to mention the greater the number of pastors that know about this, the greater the chances are that confidentiality would be violated."

The Cardinal went back to the other side of the desk, and sat down.

"The parish in our archdiocese most likely to yield a good candidate, I believe, is Old St. Pat's. That's where you find a large number of individuals dedicated to the needs of the Catholic community, generous with their time and talent, and willing to take action for the good of the Church when action is called for. And I have complete trust in you to keep this all in strictest confidence."

The very fact Father Sullivan had Cardinal Rooney's unqualified confidence made that confidence a self-fulfilling prophecy There is no way he would let him down.

"I'll need your help, Dan. You know the members of your parish better than anyone."

Cardinal Rooney and Father Sullivan then discussed the criteria defined by the Pope, and strategies Sullivan might use to target the ideal candidate. Rooney and Sullivan agreed no prospective candidate would be told what this was about until Cardinal Rooney had reviewed the candidate's suitability for the trial.

This was not the first special project the Cardinal had given Father Sullivan, but never the likes of this one – with implications not just for the parish or archdiocese, but for the entire Church. There were many programs and issues that needed attention at Old St. Pat's, but all of a sudden they faded into the background in light of this new and urgent assignment.

CHAPTER 26

Father Sullivan did have one issue he had to take care of before addressing his new assignment for Cardinal Rooney.

One of Old St. Pat's periodic weekend retreats, quite popular with the church's membership, was coming up in one week, and the lay retreat leader had just been hospitalized. Father Sullivan needed to find a substitute immediately.

He had a list of names of those who had done this before. He called the first two, but neither was available. The third person on the list was Frederick Whitaker. He had been the retreat leader on two previous occasions, and was good at it. Father Sullivan phoned him and explained his predicament. After checking his calendar, Whitaker responded:

"I'm free next weekend, so I'd be pleased to do it, Father Dan."

"Thanks, Fred, for solving my problem. I'll send you the materials and list of registrants right away."

"By the way, Dan, I want you to know I've decided to retire. There are a lot of things I've been putting off, and now I'll have the time to pursue them. Elaine and I want to spend more time together, and do some traveling. It also means I'll finally be able to get more involved in Old St. Pat's outreach programs, so please don't hesitate to call if I can be of any assistance there."

A bolt of lightning lit up Dan Sullivan's psychological sky. *Yes! Of course!*

***

Parishes usually have certain members who are indispensable to the pastor. They are his "go to" people. They are extremely generous with their time and talent, willing to take on the most challenging assignments. They always get the job done, and do it well. Fred Whitaker was one of those people.

When the cards were on the table, when it was now or never, Father Sullivan knew Fred Whitaker was a man who would come through in a pinch.

Fred and his family had been Old St. Pat's members ever since a friend invited them to visit one Sunday ten years before. The warmth, friendliness and inclusiveness of the congregation impressed them tremendously. They quickly became regulars and, once joining the parish, never looked back.

Fred, a six foot tall physically fit 62-year old, grew up in Naperville, an affluent suburb about 35 miles west of Chicago. His father was an investment banker in Chicago's financial district; his mother a high school English teacher. With an older brother and a younger sister, Fred was the middle child.

The family belonged to St. Mary Margaret Parish. Like his brother and sister, Fred went to the parish grammar school and then to Naperville Central High School. He was an unmotivated student and, except for basketball, didn't enjoy school. When he graduated from Naperville Central, he decided, much to his parents' chagrin, to join the army.

A tour of duty in Afghanistan was an awakening for Fred. He was tortured by having friends killed in battle and by experiencing the population's suffering at the hands of both the Taliban and American forces. The war drove home to him the awful truth of the old saying "man's inhumanity to man." He came back a changed person, determined to do something worthwhile with his life.

Majoring in chemistry, he graduated with honors from St. Louis University. He then went on for an MBA at DePaul University, where he met and, upon graduation, married fellow MBA candidate Elaine Stevens.

Elaine's first position after graduate school was as a financial analyst at JP Morgan Chase Bank. After two short years, she was hired by William Blair, the investment banking firm, as a senior financial analyst. However, five years later, her interests in socially significant causes led her to leave the corporate world to join the Muscular Dystrophy Association as a manager.

Meanwhile, Fred had begun his business career with the management consulting firm of A.T. Kearney. He stayed there for three years, performing assignments for a variety of companies. One client, Abbott Labs, was so impressed with Fred's work and with his academic background in chemistry, they offered him a prestigious position as a group sales manager, which he promptly accepted.

On several occasions during the next five years, he was asked to be a witness in lawsuits against Abbott, involving products his sales team was promoting. He became fascinated with the legal process and often felt the company's litigators handled these suits poorly, even when they were frivolous.

I think I could do better.

After getting his law degree by attending Loyola Law School part-time, he left Abbott and joined the law firm of Kirkland & Ellis. He became one of their most productive and accomplished litigators.

Fred was especially successful in settling cases out of court that, if tried, might well have resulted in a judgment costing his clients considerably more. As a litigator, no one was more focused, and fought harder in the courtroom than Fred. Ultimately, he became a partner in the firm.

Years of representing clients in court had convinced Fred most disputes were the result of poor communications. He believed if both parties were honest and transparent with each other from the beginning, many lawsuits would never be filed.

He established a reputation for bringing warring parties together before trial, and finding the middle path that led to a peaceful settlement. Fred thought of himself, not as just a litigator, but also a mediator.

CHAPTER 27

When the 4:30 p.m. Metra pulled into Evanston's Central Street Station, Elaine was waiting in the car for Fred. He got in, gave her a kiss, and then she drove them home.

"How was your meeting with Father Dan?"

"Strange, actually. As you know, Dan's usually a pretty happy-go-lucky guy, but, for some reason, not today. When he called and asked me to come to his office, it sounded like it might be serious. Now that I've seen him, I know it's serious, but I have no idea *why* it's serious.

"He asked me not to share our discussion with anyone. I told him you and I have no secrets – I need to fill you in. He said OK, but no one else, not even the boys. Then he proceeded to tell me exactly *nothing*!"

Elaine looked incredulous. "Nothing? What in the world did you talk about?"

"He said he's working on a special project for the Archbishop, who asked him to get some information about my background. Dan really wanted a lot of details, going all the way back to my childhood. At first I felt it was intrusive, and I was uncomfortable. Eventually, though, my curiosity got the better of me, and I told him everything I could remember. I think about the only thing he didn't ask me for was information about my toilet training!"

Elaine laughed. "I'm sure that would have made a great story!"

"At first, I thought the Cardinal might have a confidential legal problem and need my advice. But if so, why hadn't he called me directly and invited me to meet with him? Why all the questions from Dan, including – surprisingly – questions about you?"

Startled, Elaine asked "How did the meeting end?

"Dan said he'd talk to Cardinal Rooney, and get back to me. It was all so mysterious. You'd think I was being interviewed for an undercover job with the CIA. Who knows - maybe I was!"

Elaine continued driving until they reached their home on Lincolnwood Drive, where the family had lived for sixteen years. When they were first married, Elaine and Fred rented an apartment in Chicago's Bucktown neighborhood and then moved to an apartment on Lake Shore Drive in Chicago's Gold Coast area. When they moved to Evanston in 2029, they purchased their first and only home.

Fred got his usual warm welcome from Goldie, their Labrador retriever. Their oldest son, Bob, was a sophomore at Notre Dame and away now at school. Chris, a sophomore in high school, was in his room surfing the Internet. Bob was tall like his father, and Chris was getting there. Both boys were athletic, good students and leaders in most of what they did. They had a lot of their father in them.

Fred poured a drink, and had just sat down to read the mail when the phone rang. Father Sullivan was on the line.

"Fred, can you meet me tomorrow morning at nine o'clock at the Cardinal's residence?"

CHAPTER 28

The Cardinal's residence is an imposing three-story red brick Queen Anne mansion on North State Parkway, built in 1885 by Patrick Feehan, first Archbishop of Chicago. The building is often referred to as the "House of 19 Chimneys," for obvious reasons, and is listed on the National Register of Historic Places.

Fred left early for his trip down Lake Shore Drive to avoid commuter traffic. Since he arrived 20 minutes early for his appointment, he parked his car on a side street and stopped for coffee at a LaSalle Street restaurant. He showed up at the Cardinal's door five minutes ahead of time, and was greeted by Father Sullivan.

"Come on in, Fred. The Cardinal will be with us shortly."

He escorted Fred into the parlor. After they chatted for a few minutes about the upcoming retreat, he gave him a packet of materials.

"I forgot to give this to you yesterday, so I brought it with me today."

A few minutes later, Cardinal Rooney joined them, and greeted Fred warmly.

"We haven't met, Mr. Whitaker, but I've heard a lot about your fine legal work. Please sit down."

The Cardinal engaged Fred in some small talk. Then he was silent for a minute, looking at his hands folded in his lap. Finally, he looked up and said abruptly:

"Mr. Whitaker, how would you like to be a Cardinal?"

Although surprised by the question, Fred immediately assumed this was the Cardinal's way of saying "How would you like to be in my shoes, facing all the problems I do?" He expected the Cardinal would then tell him all about his latest problems, and why he was recruiting Fred to help him out.

Fred was quick-witted and had a keen sense of humor:

"I'm sorry your Eminence, I couldn't do that. You see I'm a Cubs fan, and it would be disloyal for me to get involved with the Cardinals. Besides, I don't play baseball very well. Maybe that's why I'm a Cubs fan, not a member of the team!"

Rooney and Sullivan both roared with laughter.

"This is the first time I've met you, Mr. Whitaker, but I already like you!" he exclaimed, while still laughing vigorously. "However, I'm not joking; I'm serious. Your church is asking you to be the first lay cardinal in several hundred years."

Fred was speechless! Before he had an opportunity to do much else than quietly gasp, Rooney continued:

"You and I, and everyone in the world, I imagine, know about the Apostolic Letter Pope Francis Xavier issued over two months ago, expressing his intention to elevate several laymen to the status of cardinal in order to give a stronger voice to the laity. There's been a change in that plan, Mr. Whitaker, and I want to tell you about it."

Rooney went on to explain that a number of cardinals were concerned about launching such an ambitious and drastic change in Church governance. He described their misgivings in detail, and also the Holy Father's reaction to them. The new plan, he told Fred, involves conducting a pilot program to determine whether or not it would be productive to move forward with this initiative.

"His Holiness feels the U.S. is the best place for this pilot and Chicago the best city in which to conduct it. That's why Father Sullivan and I are involved. We're looking for the ideal candidate to run the trial.

"Father Sullivan has told me about you, describing your background and accomplishments and conveying the utmost respect for you. I passed on an unqualified recommendation for you to the Holy Father. We are all in agreement you are the ideal candidate for this experiment."

Rooney paused for a moment, staring at the picture of one of his predecessors on the opposite wall, then leaned back in his chair and continued.

"Before you decide whether to accept, let me warn you. The hierarchy is not likely to give this trial any support. You've read, I'm sure, about the negative reaction when the Pope's letter was issued. To tell you the truth, I was less than sanguine about pursuing it myself. But the Holy Father instructed me to do this in Chicago, and do it well. It is my obligation to do as he wishes."

Fred was stunned. Questions raced his mind.

Am I the first candidate or the only candidate for this position? Is this a permanent or a temporary assignment? How am I able to obtain information on the attitudes of Chicago's laity? How much time would I have to complete my study and submit a report on my findings? How am I to communicate this information to the Holy See, and to the Church hierarchy?

After Fred voiced his first question, Cardinal Rooney told him he was the only candidate they had considered.

"If you accept this assignment, you will meet with the Pope in a few days and be given a lot more information."

"I am honored to be asked," Fred answered. "I clearly understand the importance of the assignment. I will need to discuss it with my wife, and pray about it."

CHAPTER 29

Fred left the Cardinal's residence with his head spinning. He felt like he had fallen down the rabbit hole, and could hardly distinguish fantasy from reality. He was being asked to be a principal player in a sea-change in the Catholic Church that would affect the lives of hundreds of millions of Catholics around the world.

Cardinal Rooney had made it sound like it would be a simple job of data-gathering and reporting, but it was clear to him this was an over simplification. He would be a bonafied member of the College of Cardinals – theoretically an equal, a peer of the other members, but not really.

Not an equal at all – the others are all ordained clergy, bishops in fact, responsible for many of the archdioceses that make up the worldwide Catholic Church.

Here is a group of men who are noted for **not** listening to the voices of the laity; and yet, this layman, albeit a cardinal, will need to argue the case to those with power and authority over the faithful, that the future of the Church is contingent on not only listening, but updating the way the Church relates to the laity so their needs are met.

I am quite sure no case I've ever presented in court was more difficult than the case Cardinal Rooney and Father Sullivan are proposing that I prepare and argue.

What would happen to the travel plans we have made for the coming summer? And even more important – what will Elaine's reaction be to my taking on this huge responsibility right after I retired so we could spend more time together?

✳✳✳

"Honey, how did it go?" Elaine asked as he entered the house. It was already late afternoon. Fred had been driving along the lakeshore down to the Indiana border and back, lost in deep thought. He stopped for a quiet lunch in Gary, and then drove the expressway back to Evanston.

"Let me tell you about it after dinner, sweetheart. I need to sort some things out in my mind first."

Elaine was disturbed. She rested the book she was reading on her lap and watched Fred ascend the hallway stairs.

This isn't like Fred. What happened? What's wrong?

Since it was a cold January evening, Fred built a fire in the living room after dinner. Chris was up in his room studying. That made the timing for their talk favorable, since Fred had promised the Cardinal he would keep their meeting confidential – sharing it only with Elaine.

"I don't know where to begin, Elaine. I guess at the beginning. I'll tell you what happened at the meeting this morning.""

Fred pulled no punches. He laid out, in detail, what the Cardinal told him, and his own responses and reactions – everything. Elaine listened quietly, but her face grew ashen as he spoke. A few tears rolled down her cheeks.

"Fred, do you realize what they're trying to do to you? They want to consign you to a fate just short of martyrdom. It's a losing proposition! The role they want you to accept is a no-win situation. The Church hierarchy is going to eat you alive – you know that's true! Like Daniel, they're throwing you into the lion's den!"

"It's not 'they,' Elaine, it's the Holy Father. And don't forget that Daniel survived – the lions never touched him."

As the evening wore on, they discussed the pros and cons, how plans for Fred's retirement would have to be postponed, how this would affect the boys. Before long both of them had shed a few tears.

Continuing to weigh the pluses and minuses, it became more clear to them that Francis Xavier's plan was, without a shadow of a doubt, terribly important – in fact, one of the most critical innovations the Church had launched in centuries. It held the promise of pumping new life into a laity that was becoming more and more disinterested and disengaged with each passing decade.

They were devout Catholics, and they firmly believed the Holy Spirit manifests itself through the courageous acts of human beings.

"I think it's my turn at bat," Fred declared. "We're going to be a team, Elaine – I can't do this without you."

"People may be talking about this moment centuries from now," Elaine declared prophetically, "calling it the time when the laity reconnected with the Catholic Church in a whole new way."

Hugging Fred, she said "Sign me up."

CHAPTER 30

Five days later they were airborne, destination Rome. The Pope had requested that Elaine accompany Fred. Father Sullivan was overjoyed when Fred called to convey his decision. Cardinal Rooney, while pleased, was less than effusive. Rooney took a different flight to Rome that day.

While they were gone, Elaine's mother was staying with Chris. Since they couldn't give their real reason for the trip, they invented a 'cover story' about the Cardinal needing Fred's expertise at an upcoming Vatican meeting.

Arriving at Rome's da Vinci International Airport mid-morning, they took a taxi to the Parco dei Principi Grand Hotel, bordering the Villa Borghese Park. Since they were not due to see the Pope until 10:00 a.m. the following day, they wanted to be in walking distance of the Borghese Gallery and Museum. On their two previous trips to Rome, they had not been able to visit the Borghese, and relished this opportunity to see its extraordinary collection of masterpieces. After a lovely afternoon there, they had a quiet dinner at the hotel's elegant Pauline Borghese Restaurant and retired early.

When Fred and Elaine arrived at the Apostolic Palace about 15 minutes before their scheduled appointment, they were taken to the Pope's sitting room. Cardinal Rooney was already there. Fred introduced Elaine to him, and they chatted for a few minutes while waiting for the Pope's arrival.

Accompanied by Sanjay Patel, Francis Xavier came in and greeted everyone warmly. He introduced Cardinal Patel, and then sat down. Francis Xavier addressed Elaine first, asking her questions about herself – where she was from, what she did, and also the ages and interests of their boys. Fred surmised, with some satisfaction, that the Holy Father put a great deal of importance on her role in this equation.

He turned to Fred:

"I've heard so much about you. I can't tell you how pleased I am you have consented to give this mission consideration. It is impossible to overstate the importance it will play in furthering a new florescence of Catholicism in the 21st century."

✱✱✱

The Pope described in detail his thinking, as outlined in his Apostolic Letter. He also discussed his meeting a few weeks before with the nine cardinals.

His demeanor reflected a man of considerable self-confidence, but clearly disturbed by the ongoing malignancy sapping strength from the body of the Catholic Church.

"There clearly is a disconnect between the Church and many of its members, and certainly with those who now consider themselves former Catholics. I see this as a crisis that has gone on much too long without being successfully addressed. I hope this experiment – creating a lay cardinal – will provide, if not a solution, as least some useful insights into where the solution lies.

"I would be disingenuous, though, if I did not call your attention to the difficulties facing this project."

The Pope then ticked off, one by one, the problems Fred might encounter:

- *Many traditional Catholics may resist this initiative, even to the point of belligerence.*

- *Members of the hierarchy may see you as a threat to their author-ity, and behave counterproductively.*

- *There may be attacks in the media, attempts to marginalize this effort.*

- *Other denominations, Christian or otherwise, may trivialize your activities.*

"At times, I expect you may feel you have taken on a thankless and hopeless task."

Fred replied: "I was often told in the past, Your Holiness, that a case I was taking to court was hopeless. However, I found the deciding factor was usually how well I fought my case – how well I argued it."

"I thought it important that you think about such possibilities before making your decision," the Pope added.

"You'll need to consider these things before you give me your final decision whether you are willing to proceed. If you do choose to proceed, I will appoint you a lay cardinal here and now, not at a consistory of the College of Cardinals, which, under the circum-stances, would be ill-advised."

Francis Xavier's comment confirmed Elaine's worst fears.

This is exactly what I was afraid of. This is a no-win situation. Fred believes he can win a case by how well he argues it, but can he really win this case when the deck is already stacked against him?

Francis Xavier added:

"I also want you to understand your appointment as lay cardi-nal is not necessarily permanent. We have only three Orders of Cardinals: Cardinal Bishop, Cardinal Priest, and Cardinal Deacon – all are ordained bishops. Unless we add a fourth Order for laymen, your designation as Cardinal will terminate when your mission has been completed or, since this is an experiment, if I die or resign before you've completed your assignment."

The Pope paused, his gaze directed – one by one - to each person in the room. Only Cardinal Rooney failed to hold his gaze.

Then he turned to Fred and said, "Mr. Whitaker, are you still willing to assume this responsibility?"

Fred and Elaine's eyes met. Elaine's eyes filled with tears, and they nodded silently to each other. "I am ready, Your Holiness."

Tears trickled down Elaine's cheeks.

The Pope stood, handed each of them a sheet of paper, and asked them, "This is a prayer I have written for the occasion. Please pray with me."

"Many times throughout his life, the Lord Jesus told his followers that, to be like him, they must give of themselves, reach out to others, to serve, not be served. His entire life was an example of service to others.

"We, his disciples, with our all too imperfect and limited efforts, strive to follow his example, to meet the many needs, heal the wounds, and bring succor to the children of God.

"Today we pray that you bless your servant Frederick who has taken upon himself the awesome task of listening to your people, assessing their needs and desires, communicating these aspirations to leaders of the Church, and in so doing, give your children hope for the future.

"May the love of God rain down on Frederick, and by his actions, in your name, may he share that love generously with all he serves in his ministry. Amen."

Then Francis Xavier came over to Fred, gave him his blessing, and said, "Congratulations, Fredrick Cardinal Whitaker!" He slipped a special ring on Fred's right ring finger, a ring he had made especially for the new Cardinal. Everyone applauded warmly.

Francis Xavier took his seat again.

"Regarding the particulars of how you're going to obtain the necessary data for this study, I'll leave the details to you. Your training and experience as a lawyer has equipped you with skills in information gathering, analysis, and evaluation, and your track record in running projects at your parish has demonstrated your ability not only to organize tasks, but also to carry them out successfully."

Albert Rooney had sat silently throughout the entire meeting. However, these last comments of Francis Xavier bothered him immensely. He shifted in his seat and was about to interrupt, but caught himself and held his tongue.

He's leaving the structure of this project totally up to Whitaker? How can we know Whitaker won't bias the results by overstating the dissident views of the malcontents? Since he is not a member of the clergy, how can we be sure he will correctly represent the views of the Church?

Rooney had made peace with the notion that it was his duty, and would ultimately be in his best interests to support the Holy Father. But he found accommodating the views and wishes of the hoi polloi within the Church's inner sanctum very painful, and worried that the Pope was not acting in the best interests of Catholicism.

"I would like this project to be completed in about eighteen months," the Pope said. "I will want you to review your results with me, and then present your report to a General Congregation of the College of Cardinals. Our Secretary of State, Cardinal Patel, will be your conduit for advising me of your progress, and will provide whatever help you need."

He turned toward Rooney with a broad smile.

"Cardinal Rooney has generously offered to make his archdiocesan offices available for support, and I know he will provide any assistance you might need. The Holy See will pay all expenses. And, of course, you will receive a salary, the details of which Cardinal Patel will discuss with you after our meeting."

Looking around the room, the Pope said, "I ask all of you to keep this meeting in strictest confidence. I will make a public announcement about the program next Sunday morning."

He went to a side table, removed several pieces of paper from a folder, gave one to each, and explained: "These are 'talking points' for the program. After the announcement is made on Sunday, all of us should use them as a guide for our remarks to the public."

"Cardinal Whitaker, it is hard to predict what the immediate reaction to this initiative will be, but we should anticipate some hostility. I strongly recommend you direct calls to your home phone number to an answering service, and that you and your family get another unlisted line for private use. For the foreseeable future, you should engage a security firm as a protection for yourself, your family, and your home. I am sure this is more vigilance than is necessary, but if we err, we should err on the side of caution."

The Pope then rose to end the meeting, but added as an afterthought, "Before you meet with Cardinal Patel, you need to see our tailor so he can fit you for cassocks and a biretta for liturgical and ceremonial occasions."

Fred began to protest, but Francis Xavier continued, "You are a member of the College of Cardinals now, and you need to dress like one! In your day-to-day activities, I expect you to wear a suit, like the one you are wearing right now, but with one small addition. I would like you to wear the lapel pin I had made just for you."

He reached in his pocket and brought out a small jewelry box with a golden lapel pin in the shape of the papal coat-of-arms, beneath which was inscribed the Latin motto *Cardinalis Populorum* (The People's Cardinal)."

The Pope stood, gave his blessing to everyone, and shook their hands. As Cardinal Patel and he were leaving, he asked Cardinal Rooney to join them, and he told Fred an assistant would be in momentarily to take him to the tailor shop.

Fred and Elaine sat alone in the room, looking at each other, holding hands. They said nothing. In truth, there were no words to express what they were feeling.

CHAPTER 31

While Fred went to the tailor shop and then met with Cardinal Patel, Elaine visited the Vatican Museum. She had been there twice before, but there was so much she hadn't seen, and a number of objects she wanted to see again. Since her mind was still reeling from the overpowering experience she and Fred had been through that morning, this visit was therapeutic and very restorative.

Fred sent her a text message on his cell phone when he left Cardinal Patel's office, and they returned together to their hotel. They had planned to go to another restaurant that evening, but neither felt like leaving the hotel, so they again enjoyed a dinner at the Pauline Borghese.

Both understood the die was now cast – Fred was an authentic Cardinal of the Roman Catholic Church. The challenges they faced seemed overwhelming.

They talked about Fred's altered retirement plans, and discussed the impact of the project on their children and other members of their families. They were also concerned about its effect on their relationships with friends. Most of all, though, they were worried about the stress this new undertaking might have on their marriage. They had survived a normal share of life's ups and down, but could their marriage survive the unique challenges that might now confront them?

Elaine was also thinking about her retirement plans. If Fred now had a job that would probably keep him even busier than his law practice, should she continue working? Or should she quit her position and use her skills to support Fred's work?

At the moment, they had no answers for all these questions. However, just airing them together brought them some relief. They were quite confident their marriage was strong and able to face whatever the future held. Clearly, they were in this together.

The next morning they boarded a flight to Chicago from da Vinci. After their discussion the evening before and a good night's sleep, they were more relaxed and accepting of the new life before them.

They saw God's hand in these new developments, and firmly believed the Holy Spirit was going to be a third party now in their partnership.

As the plane gained altitude, Elaine took out a paperback she had brought with her, and began to read. Fred looked out the window at the ground far below, lost in thought. Fred suddenly looked at Elaine and said, " I've just had a brainstorm – a brilliant idea!"

"What's that?" she asked.

"You know your friend Roberta? Well, the next time she begins telling you about her 'son the doctor,' you should tell her about 'my husband, the Cardinal!' "

CHAPTER 32

"Monsignor Martin Ramsey is here to see you, Your Eminence," Father Gustavo Bivona, Cardinal Ruggieri's secretary told him.

Ruggieri had been fretting – "steaming" would be a more apt description – about the news he received that morning. The day before, Cardinal Rooney had met with the Pope, along with his choice for the lay cardinal initiative. It was a confidential meeting – no one was to hear about it – but Cardinal Ruggieri had his sources, a network he had built over the years, and it was very reliable.

It troubled him. He would have expected Rooney to inform him the meeting was to take place, but he heard nothing. Even more disturbing – the selection for lay cardinal turned out to be a very experienced and prominent Chicago lawyer. He had specifically told Rooney to make sure the trial was not successful. Picking a "winner" for the project was not in line with Ruggieri's instructions.

Ruggieri was looking forward to seeing the Monsignor again. Years before, when he was teaching theology at the Gregorian, Martin Ramsey, then a young seminarian, was a student of his. Their views on the Church, and concerns about the damage wrought by progressive trends, were similar. A mentoring relationship developed, and they had kept in touch ever since. Ramsey was now director of the Evangelical Commission for the Diocese of Orange in southern California.

He stood and greeted the Monsignor: "Martin, it is so good to see you. Please have a seat. Your email said you were coming on a pilgrimage. A pilgrimage? In winter?"

"Good to see you, Your Eminence. Yes, a pilgrimage in winter *is* unusual," Ramsey agreed. "However, a travel agency in Los Angeles was developing a winter tour that promised a member of the clergy as leader, as well as a tour guide, for customers who like off-season rates. They invited me to be the clerical leader, and I was delighted. For doing this, they pay my way."

"Excellent! You also said in your note you had something important to talk to me about."

Monsignor Ramsey nodded, and began his narrative:

"As you know, since Vatican II, a number of traditionalist groups have emerged, some not in such good standing with the Church, and some that have been embraced by Rome. They have one thing in common: while they complain a lot about the liberal trends in the Church, they have done nothing to turn them around.

"As part of my official responsibilities, I have met people across the country who are as disturbed by the path we are on as I am. We believe aggressive action is the appropriate way to serve the Lord. We feel it is our calling."

Ramsey went on to explain what he meant by "aggressive action."

"You know, Jesus didn't just complain about the moneychangers in the Temple – He overturned their tables, and took a whip to drive them out. And in Matthew, we read that Jesus proclaimed: 'I come not to bring peace, but to bring a sword.'

"My colleagues and I decided to do something about this lethargy."

He watched Ruggieri closely for a reaction before proceeding. Something in Ruggieri's posture told him his words were not unwelcome.

Ramsey's demeanor now became more serious. He clasped his hands under his chin, and continued:

"We have formed what we call the Ecclesia Vera Society – the True Church Society. It is, and will continue to be, secret and anonymous. So far, we have cells with several members in southern California, San Francisco, Chicago, and Philadelphia."

He leaned forward, with his elbows on his thighs, and lowered his voice.

"We are keeping information about our existence closely guarded, since the actions we take sometimes may not . . . ah . . . sit well with the Church, or civil authorities. For that very reason, we only share our objectives among our cells, not the methods each cell uses to achieve them. That way, should one cell get in trouble with the powers that be for the actions it is taking, the other cells are not aware of these actions, and therefore are not implicated.

"Our objective is to do our small part to bring the Church back to its sacred roots, to what it was before Vatican II. Actions we take may be, for some, hard to understand."

He paused, put his hands in his lap. A small smile appeared on his lips, then disappeared.

"I felt you would sympathize with, and approve of, our position, Cardinal Ruggieri. I expect you may have ideas of how we, in America, can help bring Holy Mother Church back to the purity and discipline it had before that disastrous Church council 80 years ago."

Knitting his brow and lowering his eyes, Ruggieri fiddled with the pen on his desk. Finally he looked up at Ramsey.

"I applaud the courage you and your associates are showing. Your wisdom has grown with time, Martin. It sounds to me that your agenda is risky, but you are aware of this. There may be something you can do, and soon. You recall the Holy Father's Apostolic Letter last September?"

"I found it beyond belief, Your Eminence!" Ramsey responded. "Most of his proposed actions would be very detrimental to the Church, especially his scheme to give the laity a voice in the halls of Church governance."

"Indeed, Martin. I am pleased to say he has postponed the establishment of an Order of lay cardinals. Unfortunately, however, he has appointed a single one – just yesterday – as a trial in Chicago. I don't want to see this trial succeed."

The Monsignor was quick to respond: "Ecclesia Vera has members in Chicago, Your Eminence. What can we do?"

"Do what you can to undermine the success of this trial. I had hoped Chicago's Cardinal Rooney would take that responsibility, but sad to say, he is not proving reliable. The name of the lay cardinal is Frederick Whitaker, and his appointment will be announced on Sunday."

"I'll call Chicago today, Your Eminence. You can count on us!"

CHAPTER 33

When Fred and Elaine returned from Rome, Elaine went to her office the next day for meetings, and Fred gave attention to the security precautions the Pope had recommended.

Several times, during his law practice, clients of his needed their incoming phone calls screened, a new unlisted phone number, and the protection of a security detail, and Rachel Fischer, his former executive assistant, had taken care of this for him.

Kirkland & Ellis still considered him part of the team, had appointed him "of counsel," and would occasionally tap his wisdom on certain cases. K&E even had office space available for him if he needed it. So he called Rachel and asked her if she would take care of these security arrangements for him.

"Sure, Mr. Whitaker. What prompts you to take security measures?"

"I can't tell you that right now, Rachel, but you'll know by early next week."

Slated to start late Saturday, the evening before Francis Xavier would announce the initiative, Fred worked out the fine points with the security firm, and filled Elaine in on the details. All that remained was to tell their children about the role the Holy Father had asked him to play, and how this would affect all of them.

Saturday evening was designated "Special Family Meeting" time – the first time, as a matter of fact, Fred and Elaine had set up a "formal"

101

family get-together, and the kids were wondering what they were up to. Even Goldie, their Labrador retriever, looked confused. Bob was home from Notre Dame that weekend, so the timing for an inclusive family conference was perfect.

The meeting was scheduled to begin after dinner. While Bob and Chris watched a replay of the last Bears game on TV, Elaine and Fred chatted as they cleared the dinner table. They joined the boys in the living room for the "summit" meeting.

"I think I'd better start at the end – your father is now a Cardinal of the Roman Catholic Church, and has a very big job to do."

Bob's eyes bulged. "Man, I can't believe it! How did that happen?

Chris said, "Gee, dad, that's cool!"

"Son, did you say 'cool' or 'cruel?' "

"Ah com'on, dad, I said 'cool.' "

Fred grimaced, then smiled. "I'm not sure that 'cruel' might not be the more appropriate word, Chris!"

Fred went on to describe the whole scenario, starting with the call from Father Sullivan, and climaxing at the beginning of the week, when Francis Xavier elevated him to the status of Cardinal. He told them what his assignment was, that this would be difficult and time-consuming, and they would need to postpone the vacation plans they had made for summer. He also told them about the phones and the security detail.

"When can we tell our friends about this? When will Grandma know?" Bob asked.

"The Pope will make an announcement tomorrow," Fred told them, "but, until that happens, we can't talk about this to anyone."

Both boys said they understood and would comply.

Outside two cars drove up, and the head of the security detail, Eric Johnson, got out of one of them and came to the door. Fred let him in and introduced him to the family. The detail chief went over how this would work, and what to do if they had any problems.

He then brought in six other agents – they looked over the house, and made preparations for their assignment.

Fred and Elaine went to bed, realizing today was probably the last "normal" day they would enjoy for some time.

CHAPTER 34

The next day, the family drove down the Edens and Kennedy Expressways, turned off at Jackson, east to Jefferson, north to Adams, and west to Old St. Pat's for the 11:15 Mass, their usual Sunday service. Often Fred and Elaine were assigned as Lectors or Eucharistic Ministers, but weren't scheduled this Sunday.

"So far, this is a normal Sunday," Fred commented. Then he laughed. "Maybe the Pope will forget to make the announcement for a few days – that's OK with me!" He had the radio tuned to the news, but there was nothing about the lay Cardinal. He was quite sure that, when the announcement was made, it would get wide coverage.

Fred parked their car in the lot cattycorner from the church. After entering, they went to a pew on the front left side of the church where they usually sat. Typically, parishioners sat in the same section of the congregation every Sunday, so the Whitakers knew most of the people around them.

Father Sullivan was presiding at this Mass, and the Whitakers were pleased – his homilies were usually very good and meaningful.

Dan Sullivan finished reading the Gospel, but before he could start his homily, one of the ushers rushed up to the ambo and handed him a note. He read it, looked up at the congregation, and broke into a broad smile.

"I have some important information to share with you about a significant honor that has been bestowed on a well-known member of our congregation."

Fred slumped against the back of the pew. His shoulders dropped.

This is it! The Pope has made the announcement! This whole thing will now take on a life of its own!

"I am pleased to tell you Pope Francis Xavier has just announced that Fred Whittaker, whom many of you know, has been appointed a lay Cardinal, the first time this has happened in many centuries. Won't you come up, Fred, and tell the congregation what this is all about?"

Damn!

This is the last thing Fred wanted to do. He knew the talking points Francis Xavier had given him, but he was hardly prepared for a presentation.

As he walked up to the ambo, the congregation rose to its feet, applauded vigorously, and even cheered. Dan Sullivan shook his hand, and turned the ambo and microphone over to him. He waved, and they cheered louder. He held out the palms of his raised hands to signify "silence" or "enough," but the ovation continued for about 20 seconds more.

When the crowd was quiet, Fred looked over the congregation. He smiled and said, "You know, a funny thing happened to me on the way to church the other day."

There was laughter, and more applause.

The story he told them is one he would repeat, over and over again during the next few weeks:

"The Pope is troubled by the fact that many of the laity are not having their concerns addressed adequately, and he firmly believes this is adversely affecting the vitality of the Church, even driving some away, and frustrating many others."

Many faces in he congregation were smiling, and heads were nodding in approval. Fred continued:

"In the past, the Church has tried to deal with this problem, but with very little success. His Holiness believes this is the time for creative solutions. One that hasn't yet been tried – amazingly – is to find out what the people in the pews *really* think and want. What a novel idea!"

(Considerable laughter)

"He also wants to know what has prompted so many people to leave the Catholic Church and go elsewhere.

"But this information – what the faithful think and want – has to somehow make its way to Church leadership. And this is where lay cardinals come in – cardinals of the people, spokesmen for the laity.

"My appointment is an experiment. And Pope Francis Xavier thinks Chicago is the ideal place for this experiment. Will it work? I think it will!"

The congregation applauded enthusiastically.

"You're probably asking yourself, 'why did the Holy Father choose Fred Whittaker for this job'? I've been asking myself the same question, since I hardly feel equal to the task.

"Then I remembered what one of my professors at St. Louis University told me when I said the assignment he gave me was too much to expect. 'Fred, if God, in the hands of Samson, could destroy 1,000 Philistines with just the jawbone of an ass, think of what He could do with the complete ass!' "

Much laughter, applause, some standing again. Fred finished his remarks:

"I'll be asking you for help. I need to find out your concerns, and what's on the mind of Chicago's entire Catholic community. Rest assured, you'll be hearing more from me. In the meantime, keep me in your prayers – I really need them."

He returned to his pew, to a rousing standing ovation. Those seated near him shook his hand, patted his back, and hugged him.

Father Sullivan decided not to give his prepared homily – hardly a surprise. He congratulated Fred, underscored the importance of this initiative, and said the Pope had clearly picked the right man. He assured Fred that Old St. Patrick's Church was behind him 100%.

The Eucharistic celebration followed, and Communion. Father Sullivan gave the final blessing, and dismissed the congregation.

This was a far cry from the Sunday service the Whitakers were used to, or expected. What they didn't know was the excitement for the day was just beginning.

CHAPTER 35

The Whitakers joined the crowd in the side aisle wending their way to the church doors in the rear. From the opposite direction, one of their friends came pushing through against the flow, waving at them to get their attention. "Fred," he said, "there are two TV network trucks in front of the church, and several guys that look like reporters. Thought you'd better know."

Fred and Elaine stared at each other for a few seconds. Fred turned to Bob. "Here are the car keys, Bob. Get the SUV, and bring it by the rectory door. We'll be watching for you."

Bob continued for the church doors, while Fred, Elaine and Chris turned around and walked toward the sanctuary. They went behind the altar, and through the door leading into the rectory, and on to the rectory's front door. Fred stationed himself at a window so he could see the car when Bob arrived.

In about five minutes, Bob pulled up in their SUV, and Fred, Elaine and Chris headed down the rectory steps to the sidewalk and the car. As they got in, Fred noticed two men in the parking lot pointing at them, getting into a silver car, and driving toward the rectory.

"Let's go, Bob," Fred said. "For some reason, two guys may be after us."

The car accelerated with the tires screeching, and Bob sped down Adams Street to the Kennedy Expressway entrance. The silver car kept following.

Bob entered the expressway, and stepped on the gas. The silver car also sped up. Bob weaved in and out of the traffic, speeding up whenever he had a chance.

"Careful Bob," his mother exclaimed. "You don't want to have an accident!"

Bob ignored this and raced ahead – 60, 70, 80 miles per hour, cutting in and out of traffic, pounding the horn so no one got in his way. The silver car was close behind him.

He left the expressway at Peterson Avenue, some distance from their usual turnoff at Dempster, and drove east.

"Do you know what you're doing?" Fred asked him.

"Trust me, dad."

They came to a traffic light, and it was red. Bob looked both ways, and drove through it.

"Damn it, Bob. What the hell are you doing?"

"Don't swear at your son," Elaine admonished him. "Besides, cardinals aren't supposed to talk that way!"

The silver car stopped for the light, but it changed right away, so Bob's ploy didn't work.

At the end of the next block, Bob made a quick left turn down a side street. It was vacant and he barreled ahead, then a sharp right turn at the next block. The silver car was still on his tail. In two blocks, he came to a one-way street to the right, and turned left.

"God almighty, you're going to get us killed, Bob!" his father shouted.

"There are no cars on the street, dad."

The silver car came to a stop at the one-way street, and then, after hesitating, followed the Whitakers the wrong way.

Bob whipped along for two blocks, turned left, then right at the next block, then right again. No sign of the silver car.

Bob made several other turns, but basically kept going east until he arrived at Sheridan Road at the lakefront. He turned left and drove up Sheridan to Evanston.

Fred began to relax. "You knew where you were going, didn't you, Bob? How did you know that?"

"Remember, dad – I was a pizza delivery guy last summer. I know that part of Chicago like the back of my hand!"

As they were about three blocks from their home, they could see a huge crowd on their block – TV network trucks, other cars, people on foot, and an Evanston police car blocking the street. Fred pulled out his cell phone and called the number the security detail head had given him.

Within a minute, he saw Eric Johnson approach the police car, and talk to the officer. The car turned on its flashing lights, and instructed the crowd over its broadcast speaker:

CLEAR THE STREET! TRAFFIC IS COMING THROUGH! EVERYONE IN THE STREET GET ON THE SIDEWALK RIGHT AWAY!

Bob drove the car to their house. Security men had cleared their driveway of people; Bob drove into the garage, and closed the door behind them.

Fred breathed a sigh of relief. "Bob, I must hand it to you – you lost that guy, and you got us home safe and sound."

Chris chimed in: "That was awesome, bro, real cool!"

CHAPTER 36

Fred, Elaine and Bob were totally stressed-out. Chris, however, was thoroughly energized – a super car-chase, he thought, better than an action movie.

Security chief Johnson sat with them in the living room. "What happened?" he asked.

They described the morning's events, starting with the realization that the media was waiting outside the church for them, continuing with their attempt to escape from the silver car chasing them, and finally, Bob's successful strategy to lose their pursuers.

"Who could possibly want to follow us like that?" Elaine asked.

Johnson inquired, "Did you get the license number of the vehicle?"

"No, we didn't," Elaine and Fred said in unison.

"But," Fred noted, "we did notice two men were in the silver sedan."

"I got a good look at the car." Chris added. "It was a Mercedes."

"It's probably nothing to worry about," Johnson concluded. "The press is all over the place. Probably some reporters were hoping for an exclusive interview and pursued you in a 'paparazzi chase,' so to speak. It does remind us, though, that you are all going to have to be extra careful – now and until your elevation to cardinal is out of the news cycle."

"How do we get rid of the mob?" Fred asked, parting a living room window drape to look at the throng outside.

"There are dozens of media people out there who aren't going anywhere until they get a story. The best way to get rid of them, Cardinal Whitaker, is for you to go out and make a statement – tell them as much as you can."

After agreeing to do this in half an hour, Fred went into his study to look over his talking points and prepare some brief remarks for the crowd. Eric Johnson went outside and announced to the crowd that Cardinal Whitaker would speak to them shortly. He ordered his security detachment to cordon off a small area by the front door for Fred.

At the appointed time, Fred went out and greeted everyone. He described his new mission in very simple terms, making sure he stayed on message. He then offered to answer a few questions.

One reporter asked him, "How are you going to get information on the attitudes of Chicago Catholics, Cardinal?"

Fred responded that the details had yet to be worked out.

"Is this going to change the way the Catholic Church is organized?" asked another reporter.

"As far as I know," Fred answered, "no changes are anticipated. The purpose is to make sure the concerns of the laity are recognized, and taken into consideration. And as I said earlier, this is a trial – it may be expanded, or it may be a one-shot deal."

After this first "press conference," the family had an early dinner so Bob could drive back to South Bend and get a good night's sleep before his classes the following morning. Johnson had a member of the security team follow Bob's car until he was safely on the expressway going south.

"Already the crowd outside has thinned out considerably," Johnson observed. "I bet there will be few, if any, media people here in the morning. You may get requests, though, to be interviewed on morning talk shows. I suggest you make yourself available for those interviews. They will help hasten the media losing interest in your story."

Fred followed Johnson's advice and appeared on four different talk shows the following two days. As a result, media interest did wane dramatically. However, as an extra precaution, for the first two weeks after the Pope's announcement, Johnson assigned security to accompany family members on all their forays outside the house.

Following up on Cardinal Rooney's suggestion, Fred also contacted an official at the Archbishop Quigley Center (archdiocesan headquarters) for an office, clerical help, and access to assistance from the Information Technology Department, as needed. Two days after the car chase, he moved into his new office and began to focus entirely on one issue:

There are more than two million Catholics in this Archdiocese. How in hell can I ever find out what they are thinking?

Chapter 37

Professor Barkley Sylvester was on the verge of retirement. He had taught industrial psychology for most of his career – over 45 years – as a faculty member in DePaul University's MBA program.

In the past, his research and publications on the human side of enterprise were considered cutting edge, and he was a recognized leader in his field, a sought-after consultant. Now his publications were rarely cited, and refereed journals were no longer interested in publishing his articles. Today few in the field even knew his name.

It was clearly time to move on.

It was a welcome surprise for him then to get a call from a former student, especially from one of his favorites, Fred Whitaker. Fred had been a student of his in the MBA program – a real scholar – and two years after his graduation, Sylvester had worked with him as a contractor when Fred was a management consultant.

Not many of his former students or business associates ever got in touch with him any more, so a call from Fred was most welcomed. Today's call, though, was a special treat, given Fred's new position. At the end of the call, they agreed to get together the next morning.

When Fred arrived at his office, Sylvester welcomed Fred with a broad smile: "I've been reading a lot about you, Fred, or should I now call you 'Your Eminence?'"

" 'Fred' will do just fine, Barkley," Fred responded with a laugh. "This prestigious title is supposed to make my new task go smoother by eliciting cooperation from others. Whether that works or not, only time will tell. Right now, the job I have to do appears overwhelming. And a huge amount rides on the successful completion of my assignment."

"Specifically, what is your 'assignment?' "

"As you know," stated Fred, "Catholics have traditionally been raised from childhood to follow the rules and regulations of the Church. Not to do so, they were taught, is sinful."

"What I vividly remember," added Sylvester, "were the 'rules and regulations' prescribed by the nuns who taught me. We were in trouble if we broke them. They threatened to put the infraction on our 'permanent record.' My permanent record must have been a mile long!"

"I think you turned out OK, Barkley," Fred quipped.

"By and large, devout Catholics followed the guidance of the Church," Fred continued. "And even though, as they matured, they were able to make distinctions between what is really important and what is not all that significant, they usually continued to follow the customs and practices they learned as children. Recently, however, things have changed."

"I get the feeling," Sylvester commented, "that many people in the Church today are more likely to pick and choose – what we now call 'cafeteria Catholics.' "

"Precisely!" Fred responded. "Many Catholics today exhibit a 'take it or leave it' attitude regarding the Church's policies and disciplines, while others follow Rome's dictates to the letter. Sometimes it seems like there are two churches under one roof.

"To complicate matters, most bishops still expect the faithful not to question or complain, but to do only what they are told. Ultra-conservative Catholics have no problem with that approach. However, what escapes the hierarchy is that a large portion of the faithful either ignore their dictates or take them with a large grain of salt.

"Too often," Fred said, "what the people in the pews are thinking and saying never comes to the bishops' attention. Church leadership rarely hears the laity's concerns, but when they do, they don't seem to give a damn."

To illustrate his point, Fred waved his arms in front of him, palms out, as if he were a bishop insisting "Don't bother me with that kind of crap!"

"Eighty years ago, Vatican II exacerbated this phenomenon, since it modified the expectations of the laity," Fred commented. "But, to this day, many bishops continue to have problems accepting the reforms required by that Church council."

"You certainly define the problem well, Fred. So you're going to change all that?" Barkley Sylvester asked facetiously.

"Don't I wish!" Fred replied. "The Holy Father is anxious to get to the root of this crisis and is seeking answers to important questions, such as: 'What is the laity thinking? What do they object to? What are their aspirations? Why have so many left the Church? What will it take to get them back?'

"In other words, the Pope wants information. It's now my job to get that information on the over two million Catholics in this archdiocese and to present my findings to the highest levels of the Holy See."

Barkley Sylvester came up with the obvious conclusion:

"I suspect you want to talk to me about how you can take the pulse of Chicago Catholics and come up with an accurate diagnosis."

"Exactly," responded Fred. "I guess my intentions are pretty transparent."

"I vividly recall a similar situation when I was with A.T. Kearney, over three decades ago. We were assisting Illinois Tool Works with due diligence prior to their acquisition of Great Lakes Screw Machine Company. Illinois Tool wanted to make sure the culture and attitudes of the two companies' employees would make a good fit before they finalized the take-over. As you'll remember, we contracted with you to design an attitude survey, and you and I worked together on the project."

"We came up with some real surprises," recalled Sylvester. "It almost made Illinois Tool Works back out of the deal."

"Something similar may be needed for my project, Barkley. I've considered your type of survey versus a statistical sample. As you well know, the latter, if properly conducted, is valid; but if people don't agree with the results, they will claim the sample was not taken properly. Many members of the College of Cardinals would do just that. Your survey technique, however, is comprehensive, and avoids that danger."

"After all these years," Fred admitted, "I don't remember a lot of the requirements and procedures for the process. In fact, I'm not sure whether or not it will meet my requirements. What do you think?"

Barkley sat back in his chair, took a deep breath, and let out a huge sigh.

"To survey such a large and diverse population is a mammoth undertaking, but it's doable. Let's get started."

CHAPTER 38

"We'll start by exploring this whole process – from beginning to end – and figure out what will work best for you," Sylvester began.

"First and foremost, you need to determine which issues you want to survey. I expect there are hundreds of issues Catholics today have, some are pressing and some are not. I think you should define the pressing issues and begin with them. What do you think?"

"That's absolutely right," Fred responded. "Some people think the priest should sing the end of the Eucharistic Prayer, others think he should recite it. This is a very small issue for a very small number of the faithful. No one has left the Catholic Church because of it. So how would you define the issues?"

Like the academician that he was, Sylvester got up, picked up a marker, went to the whiteboard on the wall, and started writing:

PHASE #1: INITIAL EXPLORATORY INTERVIEWS

He turned toward Fred and began to explain: "For Phase One, you should start by interviewing a small handful of people whom you know are conservative, and another group whom you know are liberal or progressive. Doing this will help determine the universe of likely issues for your survey. These interviews should be open-ended and unstructured – anything goes – and can be done one-on-one, or in a group setting, like a town hall meeting." Sylvester continued writing:

PHASE #2: STRUCTURED INTERVIEWS

He put the marker on his desk and sat down. "Based on the results of Phase One, you'll need to devise some questions to ask a larger sample in one-on-one interviews. The sample in Phase Two should include representatives of all relevant segments of the affected population: men and women; old and young; married and single; Caucasians and non-Caucasians; straight and gay; lower, middle, and upper classes socially as well as economically – all the groups you want to make sure have a voice in your study.

"Obviously, all of the interviewees will be part of more than one group. That's OK. Your objective is to make sure you have identified the appropriate segments needed for a valid opinion survey."

"These interviews, of course, are not the survey," Fred commented.

"No, they're not," Sylvester stated, as he picked up his marker and returned to the whiteboard "Now you'll have the issues from which you can craft a survey form."

PHASE #3: CONSTRUCTION OF THE SURVEY

Sylvester went on, "Phase Three is putting together a survey form for the entire Chicago Catholic population. In designing the form, make sure you express the issues as statements."

He then sat down at his computer and, after spending a few minutes typing, printed out two sheets of paper. He gave one to Fred.

THIS COMPANY WELCOMES CONSTRUCTIVE OPINIONS FROM ITS EMPLOYEES.

Strongly Disagree	Disagree	Neither Agree Nor Disagree	Agree	Strongly Agree
☐	☒	☐	☐	☐

THIS COMPANY SHOULD SPONSOR AN EMPLOYEE SOFTBALL TEAM.

Strongly Disagree	Disagree	Neither Agree Nor Disagree	Agree	Strongly Agree
☐	☐	☐	☐	☒

"Which of these results would you put the heaviest weight on, Fred?"

"I would say the softball team. The respondent strongly agrees, but only mildly disagrees about the company welcoming employee opinions."

"Understandable conclusion. Now let me add another scale:" He handed the second sheet of paper to Fred.

THIS COMPANY WELCOMES CONSTRUCTIVE OPINIONS FROM ITS EMPLOYEES.

Strongly Disagree	Disagree	Neither Agree Nor Disagree	Agree	Strongly Agree
☐	☒	☐	☐	☐

Very Unimportant	Unimportant	Neither Important Nor Unimportant	Important	Very Important
☐	☐	☐	☐	☒

THIS COMPANY SHOULD SPONSOR AN EMPLOYEE SOFTBALL TEAM.

Strongly Disagree	Disagree	Neither Agree Nor Disagree	Agree	Strongly Agree
☐	☐	☐	☐	☒

Very Unimportant	Unimportant	Neither Important Nor Unimportant	Important	Very Important
☒	☐	☐	☐	☐

"That changes the entire picture," acknowledged Fred. "The company is not welcoming the opinions of its employees, but this individual feels it's very important that it should. Conversely, he or she would like to see the company sponsor a softball team, but considers it very unimportant."

Sylvester returned to the whiteboard:

PHASE #4: ADMINISTER THE SURVEY

"The important issue in this phase," Barkley commented, as he faced Fred, "is that everyone in your targeted population gets the survey, and it is presented to them in such a way that the largest number possible is motivated to complete it and return it to you."

He turned to the whiteboard for a final time, and wrote down:

PHASE #5: ANALYZE THE RESULTS AND WRITE THE REPORT

"This is the bottom line, Fred. What does all this data mean? How do opinions differ among the various segments of the population? How do you interpret these results? What do you recommend in your final report? This opinion survey is only as valuable as the quality of your analysis and the arguments you make in the report you present to Church leaders.

"If you want me to be involved in this project, you'll first need to identify the issues, as I outlined a few minutes ago. Once you have done this, I can help you formulate the statements, design the survey form, segment the results, and evaluate them. I have the software to do that – it's all a matter of how many separate segments you want in your final report."

"I definitely want you involved, Barkley. I am confident the Holy See will pay your fee – I'll touch base with them right away. Can you believe this – I think you and I are destined to become part of Church history!"

CHAPTER 39

The session with Cardinals Rooney and Whitaker was over, and the auxiliary bishops filed out. Among them was Auxiliary Bishop Thomas Costello. The archdiocese of Chicago was subdivided into six geographic areas called vicariates, each comprising 50 to 60 parishes. Costello was Vicar of Vicariate II.

When this meeting was called, he was quite sure what it was about, and arranged to see Roméo Hayek as soon as it was over. Now that he had heard Rooney and Whitaker's presentations, his seeing Hayek right away seemed urgent.

I never thought I would live to hear what was said in that meeting! It was just short of heresy!

Costello, a Southside Irishman in his early 50s, was often described by his friends and associates as a "fair-haired boy." He was talented, and always managed to ingratiate himself with authority figures.

Others characterized him as a chronic sycophant, and two-faced. If an authority figure offered a suggestion, no matter what Costello really thought, he would always say, "That's such a wonderful idea! It reflects your wisdom. I'll do everything I can to support it."

At the major seminary in Mundelein, Costello was considered as a "comer" by the faculty, and sent to the Gregorian University in Rome to finish his studies. There he became friends with his classmate Martin Ramsey, and studied theology with Professor Antonio

Ruggieri. Over the years he kept in touch with both, visiting Ruggieri on several of his trips to Rome.

When he returned from his studies in Rome, he was assigned as associate pastor at several Chicago area churches, and then pastor at two other parishes, prior to his ordination as auxiliary bishop. His artificial sincerity and ingratiating façade had clearly contributed to his advancement.

However, Costello's assignment as a vicar was most likely as far as he would go in his ecclesiastical career. As so well described in the Peter Principle, he had reached his "level of incompetency."

Roméo Hayek, whom he was about to visit, was quite a contrast to Costello.

The son of Lebanese immigrants, who had fled Lebanon to escape the relentless harassment of Roman Catholics by the Hezbollah-dominated government, Roméo was raised in Cleveland. He was a poor example of the city's parochial school system, showing little motivation, and barely graduating from high school. After graduation, he went immediately to work in the construction industry, carrying bricks in a hod, laying and securing rebar, and other low-skilled, labor-intensive tasks.

Although he had done poorly in school, he was bright and ambitious. He honed his skills through union-sponsored training programs and advanced in the trades, eventually being promoted to foreman since he proved himself a good manager of people. Seeking better opportunities, Roméo moved to Chicago and gradually worked his way up to become the president of the Streeterville Construction Company while he was only in his mid-40s.

Hayek and Costello's paths crossed in Chicago at St. John Cantius, a traditional Catholic church that celebrates the Mass in Latin. The church was sponsoring an all-day workshop entitled "The Conservative Answer to Progressive Trends in The Church." It was at this event that Bishop Costello, one of the panelists, met Roméo Hayek, a St. John Cantius parishioner.

Their views on the Church were very much in sync, and they stayed in touch. Then, when Costello's former classmate from the Gregorian, Monsignor Martin Ramsey, recruited him as a member of the secret Ecclesia Vera Society, Costello approached Hayek, and Roméo showed enthusiasm. He was eager to participate.

CHAPTER 40

Roméo Hayek's condo was on the 23rd floor of a glass and steel high rise at 880 North Lake Shore Drive. Every time Bishop Costello visited this building, he felt he was stepping back in history. Listed in the National Register of Historic Places, the high rise was designed by famed architect Mies van der Rohe and completed in 1951. Along with its sister building, 860 North Lake Shore Drive, it was a pioneer in the modern International Style of architecture.

"Bishop, good to see you," Roméo greeted Costello as he ushered him into his living room. "You want somethin' to drink? You're lookin' mighty serious today, mad even. What's up?"

"This so-called Cardinal Whitaker's project is worse than we thought, Roméo." Costello slumped into a large overstuffed chair opposite Hayek's sofa.

"The auxiliaries just had a meeting with Rooney and Whitaker. Whitaker plans to interview a small cross-section of parishioners in five or six parishes in each vicariate, to develop a baseline of the principal issues these folks have with the Church. Then he's going to conduct a survey of *every* Catholic in the Archdiocese!"

"I hope you're puttin' me on, Bishop. This isn't how things work in the Church."

"He's already started with the first part. He's interviewed about 10 people at Old St. Pat's, his own parish, and a equal number at Holy Name Cathedral. He's going to use data from these first two sets of interviews to develop a format for the ones he plans to conduct in over 30 parishes."

Hayek slapped his forehead, and then shook his head.

"This is outrageous! What did Rooney say about this?"

Costello responded with a tone of disbelief:

"He's going to send a letter to the pastor of every parish Whitaker plans to visit, telling them the Holy Father requires this, and that Rooney expects them to cooperate."

"This is bullshit!" Hayek blurted out. "What *is* this – Church by popular vote? A 'create your own religion' game? Sort of a Vatican version of 'mother, may I?' This sure as hell's not the Catholic Church I grew up in!"

"As you'll recall, Roméo, we made a commitment to ensure this doesn't happen."

"A commitment to the super-padre, right?"

"What are you talking about – 'super-padre?'" Costello asked Hayek with a puzzled look on his face.

"You know – Ramsey. He ain't a bishop – he's less. And he ain't a parish priest – he's more. He's a super-padre."

Thomas Costello was in no mood for Hayek's weak attempts at humor.

"Monsignor Ramsey, as you well know, phoned us from Rome after his meeting with Cardinal Ruggieri, and I told him we would emasculate Whitaker's plan."

Hayek sat on the left arm of his sofa, with his arms crossed.

"I done my part, Bishop. I got a special team of 'heavies' I can count on. Ever since Illinois passed the Right To Work Law two years ago, unions try to give my work crews a bad time. These guys keep the union organizers in line, off my building sites. They're pretty rough on 'em.

"Some of my boys are real good Catholics. I got 'em to keep track of Whitaker as soon as he was back in Chicago. They won't let me down. If they have to, they'll cut 'im off at the knees!"

"It's our duty to the Holy Roman Catholic Church, Roméo, to make sure Whitaker's ungodly exercise is terminated before it gets momentum. However, we must avoid violence. That's a last resort."

"You let me worry about how to handle this, Bishop. I know what I'm doin'."

CHAPTER 41

After the initial interviews at Old St. Pat's and Holy Name, Fred identified – with Cardinal Rooney's advice and help from the Archdiocese Information Technology Department – three parishes in each vicariate for the initial interviews. These parishes represented, as much as possible, the diversity of the Archdiocese.

"Keep in mind, Cardinal Whitaker," Rooney advised him, "these pastors, as well as their congregations, are participating in an unprecedented activity, and they may be very ill at ease. Be sensitive to this, and reassure them their participation will – in no way – adversely affect their relationship to the Church."

"Thank you for the reminder," Fred responded politely to the gratuitous advice, inwardly resenting Rooney's pointing out the obvious. "I am aware this undoubtedly will be the case with some, and have tailored my remarks with that in mind."

A letter was sent from Cardinal Rooney to each pastor, explaining the project, its importance, and eliciting their help in selecting a diverse group of five individuals for Fred to interview. He pointed out that Fred would also meet with five other parishioners, who volunteered to discuss any Church-related issues that were on their minds.

The letter also expressed Fred's desire to attend an open parish meeting, prior to the interviews, where he would explain the project and the important role participating parishes would play in it.

Each auxiliary bishop received a copy of all the letters sent to pastors in their vicariate.

To kick off Phase Two of the project, Fred chose Immaculate Conception parish in the northern suburb of Highland Park, part of Vicariate I.

Days in advance of the parish meeting, Fred drove to Highland Park to speak with Father Pelton, the pastor. They went over the list of interviewees whom Pelton had lined up for Fred, and planned the agenda for the parish meeting, which was to be open to anyone who wished to attend.

Father Pelton was very cordial and cooperative. "It's hard for me to believe this is finally happening, Cardinal Whitaker. Had this initiative taken place a decade ago, perhaps the 100 parishioners we've lost in the last 10 years would still be part of the fold."

Fred was grateful, and relieved that Father Pelton was so welcoming. He was sure he would meet some resistance along the way, but he was glad the project wasn't starting off on that note.

A 7:00 p.m. parish open meeting was planned for two weeks from the date they met.

Elaine planned to go with him to the parish meeting. After his initial preparatory interviews at Old St. Pat's and Holy Name, this was the big kick-off for the project, and she wouldn't have missed it for the world.

Security head Johnson asked Fred if he wanted him to go with them. Since it had been almost a month since Fred and Elaine had returned from Rome and things were going well, Fred had reduced the security detail, and was considering ending it entirely.

"I don't think so, Eric. The seas have certainly been calm, and I don't foresee any squalls on the horizon, thank God!"

Fred and Elaine left home at 5:30 p.m. to give themselves ample time, with commuter traffic, to get to the church for the 7:00 p.m. meeting. Their plan was to go out for dinner afterwards in Highland Park at a restaurant which they knew and liked.

Father Pelton met them at the rectory. They chatted for a few minutes in his office, giving him a chance to know Elaine. Then Fred and Father Pelton talked about the presentation, and he reviewed with Fred what he planned to say in his introduction.

The three of them went to the church at 6:50 p.m.. There were already 50 people in the sanctuary – a larger crowd than Father Pelton had anticipated. The audience included most of the parishioners who were scheduled to meet with Fred in the days to come. Father Pelton went up and greeted the congregants and introduced Fred and Elaine to them. Then he and Fred went to the sanctuary, where a table and two chairs had been set up in front of the altar, and sat down.

Father Pelton started his introduction: "I know, by this time, everyone in Northeast Illinois knows who Cardinal Whitaker is. Did I say 'everyone in Northeast Illinois?' I should have said everyone in the United States, if not the world. He is undertaking a project Pope Francis Xavier personally requested, and we are privileged he is starting it at Immaculate Conception. Let me say a few word about his stellar background. He grew up in . . . . ."

Pelton was interrupted with shouts from the back of the church.

SATAN! SON OF THE DEVIL! YOU ARE TRYING TO DESTROY THE CHURCH!

Gunshots rang out! Father Pelton screamed "Everyone get down on the floor!"

Three men wearing ski masks, fired more gun shots wildly, spraying the inside of the church with pistol fire, blasting out stained glass windows. People were shrieking, sobbing. Cries of terror filled the nave:

"God help us!"

"Oh, my God!"

"Jesus, Mary and Joseph, help us!"

Then - almost before it began - it was over. The gunmen were gone. Father Pelton and Fred leaped to their feet and ran to help the injured. Amazingly, no one was hurt, not even scratched! Pelton had a minor flesh wound in his left shoulder, which proved to be from a ricocheting bullet. Many were crying, hugging each other, trying to pull themselves together, and calling their families on their cell phones. Incredibly, no one seemed to be targeted by the gunmen.

Meanwhile, the three gunmen had gotten into a silver Mercedes, parked two blocks away, and had driven off.

CHAPTER 42

Fred went over to the pew where Elaine had been sitting. She was half on the floor and half on the kneeler, with her hands over her head, making no noise, trembling uncontrollably. Fred eased her to her feet. "It's OK, sweetheart. It's over! I don't think anyone was hurt."

The police and paramedics arrived. While the shooting was going on, someone in the congregation had pushed the "911" button on her wrist phone, and the police and paramedics were there within five minutes of the event. "It's clear," the officer in charge said to Fred, "the perpetrators were trying to scare you, not hurt you."

Some officers fanned out in the neighborhood to search for the gunmen. Paramedics double-checked for injuries, and attempted to calm those individuals who were still hysterical. Fred phoned Eric Johnson, asked him to bring a car to take Elaine and him home, and also someone to drive their car back.

Officers looked for evidence. They found spent gun shells, but nothing substantial to help them identify who the gunmen were. No discarded ski masks, no weapons left behind.

Two detectives from the county crime investigation unit accompanied Elaine, Fred and Father Pelton back to Pelton's office to question them. The Whitakers had nothing helpful to contribute. There had been no threats, nothing that might have led up to the evening's violence.

"They're crazies out there," one of the detectives commented. "Why they zeroed in on this church tonight is anybody's guess."

Fred was almost certain why the church was targeted, but, for some reason, hesitated to verbalize his thought to the Highland Park Police Department.

Eric Johnson arrived with two of his security team. One drove the Whitaker's car back. The other drove with Eric, Fred, and Elaine in Eric's car.

After fixing themselves something to eat, Fred and Elaine spent the night discussing the evening's events, and its implications. Both of them were shaken.

"I don't think this is a one-shot deal, Elaine. I think there are fanatics out there who are determined to see this project fail. They want to scare people enough so they won't participate, and, of course, scare me enough to quit. I'm not ready to quit, but they sure as hell scared me. I'm going to increase security – we can't take any chances."

Elaine was direct, firm, and unambiguous.

"Fred, you can't hold these open meetings any more! It's too dangerous for all involved. For everyone's safety, you must limit yourself to one-on-one interviews."

CHAPTER 43

The next day, the media blizzard began again. Fred, interviewed on the telephone a number of times, assured all of them his project was continuing, as planned, but without parish meetings.

Fred didn't have to worry about canceling the open parish meetings. The pastors of almost every parish scheduled for a meeting told Cardinal Rooney they wouldn't go through with them. Some pastors also said the one-on-one interviews would be too dangerous for their parishioners.

Fred sat in his study, his feet up on his desk and hands behind his head, going over in his mind all that had transpired over the past two days – two days that began with excitement and enthusiasm as he launched Phase Two of the study; and then it degenerated into unimaginable terror, forcing him to reassess how to proceed with the project.

Whatever the motivation of the gunmen, they were successful in instigating anxiety and fear, potentially damaging the mission Pope Francis Xavier gave me. I'm not going to let that happen!

Fred's ruminations were interrupted by a phone call from Cardinal Patel, the Holy See's Secretary of State.

"We heard all about what happened last night, Cardinal Whitaker. The Holy Father and I are deeply concerned for you and your family's safety. If you are having second thoughts about continuing with this assignment, we want to give you the opportunity to opt out. No one is asking you to be a martyr.

"Unfortunately, there are ultra-conservatives in the Church who will go to the same extremes as any terrorist group to make sure, not only the Church remain static in both incidental and essential matters, but also actually revert to the way it was 100 years ago.

"We feel these elements may even be in significant leadership positions in the Curia."

Cardinal Patel paused for a few seconds, and Fred was about to comment, when Patel continued:

"There is no doubt in my mind that similar forces exist in the United States. I fear your project could be seen as a major threat to their agenda and they will try to do whatever they can to make sure it isn't successful."

Fred responded, "It horrifies me to think there are fanatics in Chicago who will go to such extremes. Nevertheless, this will not stop me from keeping the commitment I made to the Holy Father. My wife supports me in this decision.

"I am beefing up our security and will make any necessary modifications to the project format to ensure everyone's safety. Please tell the Pope I am on board, and will remain so."

"Cardinal Whitaker, I am gratified, and I know the Pope will be as well, that you intend to see this through. Please continue the extra security precautions – indefinitely – for you and your family and for the sake of this important mission. Promise me that you will!"

✳✳✳

After Cardinal Patel's call, Fred spent the rest of the morning, and part of the afternoon, working with Eric Johnson on increasing security for himself and the family. While the security detail had begun with four agents on the premises around the clock, this number had been reduced a few days ago. Now it would be brought up to eight agents – twice the original level.

Fred and Elaine would also be accompanied by an agent wherever they went, hopefully without the security being overly obvious to their associates; Chris would be taken to school by security and, with the principal's approval, one or two agents would remain at the school to watch for adults who didn't belong there; and, for the first time, Bob at Notre Dame, would be given a security detail.

None of this was the way the family wanted to live, but prudence dictated such precautions, at least for the time being. Eric said he would have the augmented security team in place the next day.

Cardinal Rooney called that afternoon. Fred had kept him in the loop about his plans, letting him know what he was doing and why.

"Fred, I am terribly concerned about what happened last night, and the danger you and your family may be in."

"We're going to be OK, Albert. Our security is being beefed up, and we're taking extra precautions," Fred assured him.

Rooney gave him the names of the pastors who had opted out of open parish meetings (which was most of them) and those who had decided against even one-on-one interviews at their parishes. Fred spent the rest of the afternoon contacting the latter group to ensure them they need not worry about the individual interviews, that security measures would be taken to ensure there be no danger for anyone.

Exhausted by the events of the last 27 hours, Fred and Elaine turned in before 10:00 p.m..

The following day, Johnson had the increased security detail in place. He spoke to the principal of Chris' school about having security personnel on campus. The principal was in total agreement, and even seemed relieved, since the school had been experiencing some major disciplinary problems recently. He was hoping having private detectives on campus might help prevent them as well.

Fred and Elaine stayed home that day, still recuperating from the trauma at the church. They felt sure another day's rest would help get them back to their normal routine the following day. They also kept Chris home, since the school security arrangements were not yet in place.

"As terrible and frightening as the evening at Immaculate Conception," Fred opined, shaking his head, as he and Elaine prepared for bed that evening, "it may prove to be a blessing in disguise. We were given a clear warning fanatics are out there who will go to extremes – perhaps to great extremes – to destroy this initiative of the Pope. No one was injured, thank God, and we've been forewarned. We have now taken extra precautions and I feel our safety is now assured."

Fred was not aware that he was suffering from a sense of false security.

CHAPTER 44

After breakfast the next morning, rather than taking the train to work as she usually did, one of the security agents, Tony Salera, was going to drive Elaine to her Chicago office. Still somewhat shaken up by the violence at Immaculate Conception, she felt safer this way. As soon as he drove her car out of the garage and waited for her by the front of the house, Elaine grabbed her purse and briefcase and headed for the door.

Before she could put her hand on the doorknob, she heard a loud explosion outside. The house shuddered, the living room windows cracked, and some panes shattered and fell to the floor. Fred rushed to the door, pushed Elaine aside, and rushed out the door.

A black plume of smoke billowed from Elaine's gutted car. Tony Salera's lifeless body lay sprawled in the middle of the street. Fred ran toward him but was driven back by intense flames. Sirens wailed a few blocks away.

No other structure or person on the block had been affected. It appeared a small explosive attached to Elaine's car was responsible for gutting it and killing Tony.

The fire department, police and paramedics were there in no time. The police closed off the street on each end of the block, and strung "crime investigation" yellow tape to prevent ingress and egress.

For the next several hours, several detectives poured over the area looking for clues. They questioned the Whitakers and Eric Johnson about the sequence of events, and kept the media at bay outside the taped area.

Elaine was hysterical, sobbing and moaning, on the verge of collapse. Fred and Chris were doing what they could to calm her, but they also were shaken to the core. This tragic act of violence had left the three of them in a state of disbelief, unreality, and extreme fear.

Eric Johnson was as distraught as the Whitakers.

"How could this have happened? I thought we took every precaution to secure your property. Extra security has been on hand for almost 24 hours. Tony was a good friend of mine, an exemplary agent. And now he's gone! I can't believe it! What a tragedy!"

Besides the terrible personal loss, Eric Johnson experienced a sense of deep professional humiliation.

After a while, the lead police detective came in to tell them what they had discovered.

"We've identified the car bomb. It was a delayed action device, programmed to go off a few minutes after the car had started."

"We also know how the perpetrator – or perpetrators – got into the garage. They jimmied the small window on the rear wall and squeezed in through it."

Because there was no rear door to the garage, the security team had neglected to treat the back of the garage as having an entrance, and had not installed motion sensors there. A major oversight!

After all available evidence was finally collected, the car was taken away on a flatbed truck, the debris in the street bagged as evidence, and the yellow tape taken down. Eric Johnson met with the media and gave them a prepared statement. He ended by informing them:

"The Whitakers have been through a terrible trauma. We request that you respect their privacy at this time. They will not be available for comment."

Later that afternoon at home, Fred, Elaine and Chris discussed the situation. Elaine spoke first.

"Fred, you told Cardinal Patel you would continue with this mission, but you can't go on now! The murder of Tony Salera today changes everything! Two days ago there were gun shots at the church, but this morning there was a car bomb killing in front of our home – a bomb that was meant for you or me. The danger now outweighs any value this project may have for the Church.

"There are religious fanatics out there who will do anything to ruin the Pope's mandate, even if it means killing people. You must not put yourself – or us – in such danger. It's too high a price to pay!"

Fred turned to Chris: "Son, you're part of this family. You get to voice your opinion, too. So what do you think?"

"I agree with mom about our not putting ourselves in unreasonable danger, dad. At the same time, you made a deal with the Pope. That's a heavy duty thing.

"Also, you can bring in all the security people you want. The Pope said he'll pay for your expenses. Heck, you can hire an army if you want!

"I don't like the idea of some low-lifes telling you, and the head of the Church, what to do. Someone has do draw the line, dad!"

"The trouble, Elaine and Chris, is that you're both right. I lean toward closing the project down, and telling Cardinal Patel the objective needs to be accomplished some other way, or at some other time. Let's sleep on it."

Elaine went into the kitchen to start dinner, and Fred mixed himself a bourbon and soda. The phone rang.

"Fred, this is Albert Rooney. This morning's tragedy is unbelievable!"

"Albert, I have to tell you I'm not sure I will continue with this mission. The risks to me and my family are proving to be too great."

Rooney hesitated and then continued:

"Prior to this morning's events, I was going to call you to ask you and Elaine to meet with me. Now it is clearly urgent you do so before you make your decision. Can you be at my residence tomorrow morning at nine?"

Chapter 45

Cardinal Rooney met them at the door. "Please come in, Elaine and Fred." He brought them into the living room. "Can I have my cook Alana bring you coffee or tea, and some sweet rolls?"

After the beverages and pastries were brought in, Cardinal Rooney became very pensive, a look of sadness and exhaustion on his face, and creases of stress on his brow. He mustered his energies and began speaking:

"Fred and Elaine, I'm going to share something with the two of you, the nature of which I have never shared with anyone – never had to – but it's essential I do so now. You must forgive me if I stumble a bit, searching for words, struggling to get my thoughts together. I know what I want to say, but I am not sure how to say it. Please bear with me."

Fred and Elaine exchanged an uneasy glance. These words – tentative, apologetic, uncertain – were atypical for the Archbishop. Besides, for the first time since Fred began working with him a few weeks ago, Rooney was not wearing his sacerdotals with the Roman collar. He was dressed in slacks, a sports shirt, and a sweater. He undoubtedly dressed this way when he was not at work, but his casual clothes now added to the atmosphere of peculiarity.

"First of all, I must tell you that my heart goes out to you. I can hardly visualize what you've been through in the past 48 hours – the fear for your family's safety, the sadness over the death of that poor man from an explosion that was meant for one of you. It is beyond my imagination how this ordeal must have affected you."

"Thank you, Albert," Fred interjected. "Your compassion for us is truly appreciated. We plan to attend the funeral for that young man, and I will share your sentiments with his family."

"This isn't what I invited the two of you down here to tell you – there is much more.

"Fred, we've gotten to know each other pretty well during these past few weeks. You know I'm quite traditional, conservative, and authoritarian in my approach to the Church and to my position. In this regard, I am hardly alone. The majority of the bishops, and certainly the cardinals, are in the same category."

His voice was raspy – he cleared his throat, took a sip of his coffee, and continued:

"These bishops and cardinals find the Holy Father's elevation of a layman to the College of Cardinals and the mission he has assigned to you, not only antithetical to their concept of what the Church should be, but a threat to the power structure they're a part of.

"Since we've returned from Rome, Fred, and you began your work, you've shared with me what you were doing every step of the way. You told me what the parishioners in the interviews at Old St. Pat's and Holy Name Cathedral said to you about the Church – feedback from the laity no one has ever shared with me before. I think you could say they wouldn't dare! But you did share. And when I questioned you, I got frank answers."

Albert Rooney got up, went over to the window, and stood there for almost a minute with his hands clasped behind his back. He turned to Fred.

"You made me think, Fred. You made me question my assumptions. I'm embarrassed to say this, but - like so many in the Church hierarchy – I'm not sure I've always made a proper distinction between the Church's core dogma and teachings, and its rules and regulations which can be changed. I now realize the Church practices I'm most comfortable with are not necessarily indispensable."

Fred and Elaine looked at each other in amazement.

"There was a book written shortly before the Second Vatican Council by Hans Küng entitled *The Council, Reform and Reunion*. You may know of Küng – he was a prominent theologian, well-respected by the Church at the time, but fell out of grace due to some of his positions being considered inconsistent with Church doctrine. This book was required reading when I was in the seminary.

"In this book, Küng said something to the effect that the Church became Greek for the Greeks, Roman for the Romans, and then it stopped there. It never became German for the Germans, Dutch for the Dutch, English for the English, Chinese for the Chinese, and so forth. Much of that was changed in Vatican II."

This was an awkward situation, and Fred felt compelled to say something.

"Albert, your contributions to our Archdiocese are recognized by all as being significant, and . . . "

Rooney interrupted him, as if he hadn't heard a word Fred had just uttered.

"Did the Church, which was very relevant during medieval times stop growing and changing from that point on? Today, does it make room for those who accept Church dogma, but express their faith in different ways? Does the Church leadership always make a distinction between the fundamental and the incidental, between the teachings of Christ and customs that can be modified?

"Is the Church's tent now big enough to include those who find they can best express their faith in traditional ways and those whose idiom is more in tune with 21st century ways? What do the faithful want? What do they consider important?

"Fred, these are issues I am struggling with, thanks to the vision of our new Holy Father and the vitality you bring to your project."

"I admire you, Cardinal Rooney," Elaine broke in. "I think you are a courageous man."

"There's more, Elaine," Rooney continued. "When I was in Rome for the Conclave that elected Pope Francis Xavier, a faction of significant Church leaders – with questionable loyalty to the Pope – invited me to join them. I was shocked by this meeting, and wasn't sure how to react. They discussed protecting the Church's traditions. However, I thought they were equally worried about saving their own authority system. I came away from the meeting, having my own assumptions about what is important terribly shaken."

Cardinal Rooney paused, his eyes fixed on Elaine, and then on Fred.

"Obviously, some individuals in Chicago seem to have similar ideas and motivations. I believe they are violent and dangerous, and are out to do you harm."

"Albert, as much as I want to see this mission competed successfully, I don't want to continue to put my family in harm's way. That's too high a cost."

"I agree. But, Fred, I think there is a way for you to pursue this assignment and to minimize the chance of danger to you, your family, and others. Elaine, I invited you here this morning since I consider you to be a vital player in this decision. I know the two of you can increase family security as much as necessary, and the Holy See will pay for the cost. I have some new thoughts, though, on how we can use technology and drastically reduce the personal danger to all concerned.

"It can be done. But first, I need you both to say you're willing to proceed."

CHAPTER 46

After their two-hour meeting with Cardinal Rooney, Fred and Elaine began their drive home. Both agreed Rooney's virtual epiphany was a game-changer.

Rooney was no longer only tolerating the project – giving it just the support the Pope required – but he was now a part of the team. His vision had broadened, and for the Whitakers, to walk away from it now would not only inflict a wound on the Pope, but also on their Chicago Archbishop. Elaine and Fred came to the conclusion Fred must continue with the project.

When they arrived home, they both collapsed on the living room sofa.

"Fred," Elaine said after a few minutes of silence as she stared out the living room window, "I always knew life was uncertain, but no one told me it was a roller-coaster. No, I take that back – it's more like the 'house of horrors' at an amusement park, with the scary lights, screams and things jumping out at you. Except, at the amusement park, you know it's make-believe. This isn't."

"You know, Elaine, if I hadn't told Father Dan earlier this year that I was retiring and would have some extra time, this probably never would have happened. We would be planning our summer vacation now! Makes me think of a song from my parents' era: 'I beg your pardon, I didn't promise you a rose garden.' Well, we certainly didn't get a rose garden!"

"Do you think security has now provided us with enough agents and equipment to ensure our safety can't be breached?" Elaine asked.

"I believe they have," Fred replied. "There are now eight agents at the house 24 hours a day. Every vehicle that drives onto our block is under surveillance. All the agents are armed. Chris and Bob are well-protected. The only contingency not allowed for is an airplane that drops a bomb on the house. But I guess nothing's perfect!"

Fred and Elaine kept Bob abreast about what was happening in Chicagoland. After the shooting, and especially the car bombing, he said he was coming home, but they told him to stay at Notre Dame.

"Everything's under control," Fred assured his son. "There's nothing you can do by being here, and you'll miss lectures that may be important. We will be in touch frequently to let you know how things are progressing. Don't worry!"

Fred phoned him that afternoon to tell him about the meeting with Cardinal Rooney, and the decision he and Elaine had made to go ahead with the mission.

After talking with Bob, Fred called Cardinal Rooney. When he said they both had agreed to proceed, Rooney breathed a sigh of relief. He promised them both his unqualified support.

When Chris returned home from soccer practice about 4:30 p.m., Fred and Elaine informed him of their decision.

"That's great!!" Chris enthused. "So, no one's going to get away with pushing the Whitakers around! Wait till I tell the guys at school!"

"Chris," his father admonished him, "we'd prefer you not talk about this at school. We want to keep a low profile. It's safer that way. Try to forget the last few days even happened."

"All the kids want to know what's happening, dad. They think I've got the most exciting life of anyone at the school."

"We could all do with a little less excitement around here, Chris. Try not to keep this story alive, son. Let it die a natural death."

CHAPTER 47

The next day, Fred was off to the Archbishop Quigley Center for a planning meeting with Cardinal Rooney. Two detectives from the security agency accompanied him; one of them drove his SUV, the other rode "shotgun." Fred hated all this protection, but knew he'd better get used to it.

"Fred, you already know having open parish meetings is now out-of-the-question. I'm afraid one-on-one interviews are also all but *verboten*. Although many of the pastors support your mission, they don't want you near their churches, lest you bring trouble with you. The terrorists have indeed been successful in scaring the wits out of everybody."

"Yesterday," Fred reminded him, "you said you had an idea on how I can still achieve my mission's goals - in spite of all this."

"Yes, I do," Rooney responded.

"If my memory serves me correctly, you and the pastors at your targeted parishes have identified about 10 people per parish, or about 180 individuals, to interview in the second phase of the project.

"Two features would have made this workable: ease of communication – by having face-to-face interviews – and the promise of confidentiality, assuring the parishioners their remarks would go no farther than the four walls of the room they were in."

"That confidentiality" Fred interjected, "is absolutely essential. Given the nature of this project, anonymity and privacy must be guaranteed."

"I agree. Until recently," Rooney continued, "electronic communication couldn't meet this requirement. It had ease of use, for sure, but anyone could hack into a message and identify the sender and receiver."

"As you know, about two years ago, Congress passed the Privileged Privacy Act of 2043. Now, with federal court approval, an entity with a qualifying project can gain access to a new and totally secure network – a highly innovative technology – for use by that project only. It bypasses the usual Internet servers so messages can't be read by third parties. It has proven to be hack-proof. No one but the sender and receiver – not even law enforcement – can read these messages without a court order based on evidence of a crime."

Fred cautioned, "It's only a matter of time, Albert, before someone develops the ability to compromise this system."

"You're probably right," Rooney acknowledged, "but I understand it's going to be very difficult to do, and may not happen for several years."

"The Archdiocese already has one project approved for such a network, and it works extremely well. I'm quite sure, Fred, it would work well for your project, too, and solve your privacy problem. If it meets with your approval, I'd like to send our attorneys to federal court right away. I believe your project will be accepted, and then you can obtain the codes necessary to give you access."

Fred was quiet and pensive as he stared into space for several seconds. "This sounds like the only option that will meet our objective. Let's go with it!"

Rooney concluded:

"Why don't you draft a letter to those targeted for interviews? We'll send it over both our signatures – you as the Pope's emissary, and I as Chicago's Archbishop. In the meantime, I'll take care of getting court approval for your project."

CHAPTER 48

Fred went right to work on a letter to be sent to each of the 180 parishioners in the 18 targeted parishes. After Cardinal Rooney had his lawyers successfully petitioned for Privileged Privacy Network access for Fred's mission, the two reviewed Fred's draft and finalized it for mailing.

Each recipient received the following letter, with a copy sent to the appropriate auxiliary bishop vicar:

Dear [parishioner's name],

We want to thank you for expressing your willingness to be interviewed by Cardinal Whitaker as part of the mission assigned to him by His Holiness, Pope Francis Xavier. As you are aware, the Holy Father is determined to increase communications between Church leadership and the laity, so the concerns of the faithful are clearly heard by the local Church and by the Holy See.

Words can not express the shock and sadness we are experiencing over the violent shooting spree at Highland Park's Immaculate Conception Church, and the vicious and senseless bombing of the Whitaker's car, resulting in the death of an innocent security agent. This is undoubtedly the work of desperate, criminal individuals, who demonstrate no limits in their crazed attempts to subvert the intentions of

151

our Supreme Pontiff. Our hearts and prayers go out to the family of the security agent.

We are determined not to be intimidated by these terrorists. At the same time, we want to ensure those generous individuals who have volunteered to assist Cardinal Whitaker in this important mission are in no way put in harm's way. Since having Cardinal Whitaker interview you at your church might be a magnet for those who mean to do us harm, we have decided to cancel that part of the program.

However, we have found an entirely safe way for you to still participate in this project. As you may already know, the government launched a Privileged Privacy Network about two years go. It is a secure email system, and special permission to access it must be authorized by the courts. Cardinal Whitaker has received such authorization. He urges you, therefore, to communicate with him by email. By using his email address at the top of this letter, your message will be transmitted by the totally secure Privileged Privacy Network. It will remain confidential, and your privacy assured.

From his interviews with parishioners at Holy Name Cathedral and Old St. Patrick's Church, Cardinal Whitaker has already identified several topics on the laity's mind, including the following:

- *The selection process for parish pastors.*

- *Married clergy.*

- *The ordination of women.*

- *The role of the laity in the Church.*

- *The reasons Catholics are leaving the Church.*

- *Ways to accommodate the needs of both more conservative Catholics and more progressive Catholics.*

- *The sexual abuse of children by certain priests.*

- *The accountability of bishops and cardinals in the sexual abuse scandal.*

- *Abortion.*

- *Contraception.*

- *Divorced Catholics receiving the Sacraments.*

- *Same-sex marriages.*

You may have other concerns, different than these, which you may want to express.

There are basically two types of issues people have raised: some have to do with rules and practices which can and have changed over time, such as parts of the liturgy, and governance of he Church; others are matters of Church dogma or articles of faith which will not change, such as the divinity of Christ and His resurrection from the dead.

Feel free to express your opinions or concerns about any issue. Problems you perhaps have with articles of faith may indicate the Church can do a better job of teaching them, and explaining them.

For those of you who still want to meet personally with Cardinal Whitaker, it will be possible for you to do so. If you call the toll-free number, under his email address at the top of this letter, it will ring directly in his office, and an appointment will be made for you to visit with him at the Archdiocesan headquarters in the Archbishop Quigley Center. If you care to meet with him, let us assure you security at the Center will be exceptionally tight.

As another part of the project, we will also offer an opportunity for former Catholics to share their views with us.

It's hard to overemphasize the importance of your participation in this mission. From the information you provide, Cardinal Whitaker will prepare a survey to be distributed to all Catholics in the Archdiocese. Without identifying any participant, the results of this survey will be reported directly to the Holy Father

We ask you to send an email message or make an appointment to see Cardinal Whitaker by April 10. Thank you for your participation and cooperation.

Yours in Christ,

Albert Cardinal Rooney   Frederick Cardinal Whitaker
Archbishop of Chicago   Special Emissary of Pope
                               Francis Xavier

Rooney and Whitaker signed each letter individually.

CHAPTER 49

The ink on their signatures on the letter was hardly dry before the worldwide media was covering this important news story from Chicago. For the first time in the Catholic Church's history and, in spite of intimidation and violence from extremists, the laity were being given a chance to express their issues and concerns on an exceptionally wide variety of Church-related matters. TV news broadcasts featured interviews with Cardinals Rooney and Whitaker, and touted them as courageous and progressive Church leaders.

Elsewhere in the United States and even globally, Cardinals and bishops were also the object of media attention. Their reactions were very predictable. Only a handful expressed praise for what was happening in Chicago.

For Cardinal Antonio Ruggieri, the news from Chicago was beyond belief!

Cardinal Whitaker's assignment should be dead by now! Yet, it's thriving! Cardinal Rooney was charged with killing this initiative before it even got off the ground. He not only failed to do so, but he has become a facilitator for the project —and not just a facilitator, but a cheerleader!

Whitaker and Rooney are being lionized as brave warriors, who, in the face of mortal danger, have shouldered on!

This experiment of giving a voice to the laity in Chicago, is now known worldwide. It's re-structuring the expectations of the faithful. This is getting totally out of hand – it's unacceptable!

This situation couldn't be worse!

Ruggieri decided to take action. He picked up the phone and called Monsignor Martin Ramsey in California. Ramsey, who visited Ruggieri earlier in the year and told him about his Ecclesia Vera Society, was supposed to have his Chicago operatives end Whitaker's project. He had failed.

"Martin, this is Antonio Ruggieri. Do you have any idea why I am calling you?"

"I'm afraid I do, Your Eminence."

"You committed yourself to having your Chicago operatives stop this travesty before it got off the ground. What's going on?"

"Right after we saw each other, I talked with Bishop Thomas Costello, who heads that cell," Ramsey replied, "and he assured me they would go into action."

"And so they shot up a church and killed a security guard, and figured that would do it, right, Martin?" Ruggieri replied, spitting out the words with venom and sarcasm.

"I have no idea, Your Eminence."

"Goddamnit, Ramsey – give me a straight answer! What do you mean you 'have no idea?' "

"As I told you when we last met, Your Eminence, this is a secret society, and sometimes we may do things that are . . . ah, that are . . . that civil authorities might not totally approve of. We took an oath that each cell, Chicago being one of them, would not share with anyone – not even the other cells – the actions they are taking. That way, the 'uninvolved' cells are protected if there's trouble. We share objectives, but not the means to achieve them."

"You're telling me, Martin, you had no idea what your associates in Chicago were going to do or what they are planning to do in the future?

"As I told you, Your Eminence, we do not . . . "

Ruggieri hung up on him.

To say Antonio Ruggieri was not a good loser is a gross understatement. During his career, if he suffered a setback, he was irreconcilable, and became preoccupied with regaining his status. Any time he was outcompeted, he viewed it as a personal affront, and all his mental and psychological energy was focused on how to humiliate his adversary. You got on the wrong side of Antonio Ruggieri at your own risk. He was canny, and yes, ruthless.

As a young priest, he pulled strings to get out of parish work, and obtain a teaching appointment at the Gregorian University. When Leo XIV failed to reassign him as Prefect of the Congregation for the Doctrine of the Faith, he left no stone unturned in his efforts to get reappointed by Pope Paul VII.

However, the current situation in Chicago was beginning to stymie him. He didn't have a ready solution. He was furious.

In the past, when the stakes were high, he knew he could turn to Dieter Kaufmann, Archbishop of Munich, for fresh ideas and uncompromising support. He needed to talk to Cardinal Kaufmann, and, when he phoned him, he discovered Kaufmann's outrage was second only to his.

"What's happening in Chicago, Antonio, is disgraceful, outrageous, preposterous! Totally unacceptable!" Kaufmann blurted. "A disastrous compromise of immutable Church doctrine! Immensely damaging to Church governance! What can we do to stem this disaster?"

"It borders on criminal," Ruggieri sputtered. "Not just criminal – sacrilegious!"

"We need to take a hard look at the man who gave Whitaker this assignment, Dieter. The New Testament and the early Church Fathers tell us the Antichrist is 'the deceiver,' the one who advocates false and misleading doctrines.

"Is this Pope actually the Antichrist? If so, then how can he be a legitimate pope? We need to carefully consider these matters.

"Do you expect to be in Rome in the near future?" Ruggieri asked Kaufmann.

"I'll be coming for my required *Ad Limina* visit to update the Pope on my archdiocese in about two weeks, Antonio."

"You and I need to meet while you are here. There is no way we can let this 'voice of the laity' initiative continue to a successful completion. Be thinking about possible courses of action, Dieter. Think of everything! When we meet, every option needs to be on the table!"

CHAPTER 50

Since he and Cardinal Rooney sent the joint letter to 180 parishioners who had originally volunteered to meet with him, things had gone better than Fred expected.

He had asked them to send their comments, opinions and concerns to him by email, and to his amazement, 150 had done just that – well more than he had anticipated. And for the most part, the responses were fairly detailed and well thought-out.

Fifteen had requested face-to-face meetings with him at the Archdiocesan headquarters. Most surprising of all, 17 additional emails came from parishioners who were not part of the original group, and apparently had gotten his email address from friends.

Phase Two of my project has gone extremely well – it surpasses my expectations.

A damper was temporarily dropped on his enthusiasm by an unexpected "command performance."

The U.S. Conference of Catholic Bishops (USCCB) was having a late spring meeting, and, through Cardinal Rooney, had requested Fred attend and tell them what he was doing. Giving a presentation to the USCCB was not part of his game plan, and Fred was not comfortable with the prospect. He expressed grave misgivings to Rooney.

"Albert, this sounds like they plan to put me on the defensive, maybe even try to torpedo my efforts. I think this is imprudent, and I have no desire to put my hard work at risk."

"I see your point-of-view, Fred, but I don't think you should turn this down. If your project is the success we think it will be, the Holy Father is going to expand the effort, and you'll have to sell it, not only to the College of Cardinals, but to many other members of the Church hierarchy.

"This is sort of like Moot Court, when you were in law school."

Fred grimaced: "I hope not!"

"Actually, this could be a golden opportunity" Rooney continued. "You can explain to them your procedures and methodology, but no one will challenge your results – as yet, you don't have any! That's months away, wouldn't you say?"

Fred reconsidered.

"I guess I could consider this as a dry run for the 'Big Show' in Rome, Albert. Very little's at stake right now."

Fred phoned Cardinal Patel in Rome, and he agreed with Rooney's assessment.

Rooney was staying at the Radisson Plaza-Warwick Hotel where the meeting was being held, but he and Fred agreed it would be better for Fred not to stay there, to just show up at the prescribed time for his presentation.

Fred arrived at the Courtyard Philadelphia Downtown Hotel late afternoon. That evening, he spent some time going over his notes, and a PowerPoint presentation he had prepared.

I know how to make a convincing argument in front of a jury, so tomorrow shouldn't be much different. And I have all my ducks in a row.

***

The next morning, Fred took a cab to the Radisson for his 11:00 a.m. presentation. Since he planned to take a flight back to Chicago that afternoon, he brought his suitcase with him, and checked it at the front desk. He went to the room where he was to speak and made sure a computer and projector were in place for his presentation.

When it was time for Fred to speak, the USCCB president, Frank Koys, Archbishop of Portland, Oregon, introduced Albert Rooney who, in turn, introduced Fred:

"Brothers, it is my pleasure this morning to introduce you to Cardinal Frederick Whitaker. As you know, Cardinal Whitaker has been given an unique assignment by our Holy Father – the importance of which for our Church's future is, at this time, beyond our ability to fully comprehend."

Rooney went on to review Fred's career as an outstanding businessman, lawyer, and contributor – of both time and talent – to his parish. He noted especially his willingness to take on the challenging and difficult task Pope Francis Xavier had assigned him. He then turned the floor over to Fred.

A small sprinkling of polite applause followed Fred as he stepped to the podium.

He looked out over an intimidating sea of black suits and Roman collars. About 200 bishops, archbishops and cardinal archbishops faced him. Apparently this was an unusually large turnout for a mid-year meeting of the USCCB, probably because they wanted to hear what the lay cardinal had to say. This realization relaxed Fred a bit.

Since they're here specifically to learn some details about my assignment, I'll assume I'm a welcome guest. Still, there is no doubt I am appearing before a very formidable jury.

He began, addressing the Conference president:

"Your Excellency, and your assembled Excellencies, I am deeply honored for this invitation to bring you up-to-date on the mission assigned me by our Holy Father. Although it will be some time before we have definitive results from this effort, I am pleased to share with you our progress so far, and the methodology we are using in the process."

Fred found a little humor at the beginning of a presentation usually proved to be an effective "warm-up" for an audience, so he proceeded:

"First of all, you may be asking yourselves how it came about that I was chosen for this assignment. I'm sure you all remember the comedian/actor/director Woody Allen who was so popular in the 20th and early 21st centuries. He once said '80% of success in life was just showing up.' Well, I showed up, and the result was hardly what I was looking for, to say the least."

Fred expected a few laughs for this light hearted lead-in to his presentation. Not a laugh. Not a giggle. Not even a smile. Nothing but steely stares from the massive assembly of black suits in front of him.

He had a couple of other amusing and playful comments to make before he launched into the body of his talk, but he scratched them entirely. This was without a doubt a hostile jury, and he hadn't yet presented his opening arguments!

***

Fred launched his PowerPoint presentation. As he addressed his audience, he underscored the worldwide dimensions of the problems facing the Church, especially the pervasive influence of secularism.

"Over the past few decades, the Church has been experiencing a series of troubling phenomena that has eaten away at the very substance of Catholicism."

He advanced to a slide enumerating the challenges facing the Church:

- *Why have some left the Church and embraced Pentecostal movements?*

- *Why has Sunday Mass attendance continually declined among individuals who identify themselves as Catholics?*

- *Why do young people increasingly find the Church irrelevant?*

- *Why do good, upstanding and ethical church-goers freely admit they are 'cafeteria Catholics?'*

- *Why do some conservative and traditional Catholics feel they no longer have a home in the Church, and form break-away congregations that Rome is not able to sanction?"*

His eyes – with considerable intensity – slowly scanned the assembly:

"We need answers to these questions – answers that will enable us to address such troubling phenomena effectively, and begin reversing these trends. We need to know what is truly on the minds of the laity."

Auxiliary Bishop Allen Millard of Lincoln, Nebraska couldn't wait for the question-and-answer period at the end.

"Mister Whitaker," he addressed Fred, as an obvious slight, "I am well-aware your background is . . . light . . . in theology and Church history," he continued with an unctuous and supercilious tone of voice. "I am afraid you have very little understanding of the Church's governance and magisterium.

"The holy Catholic Church has been around for over 2,000 years, and has done a pretty good job of leading the faithful on the road to salvation. It has followed the dictates of Jesus Christ to the letter.

"It may come as a surprise to you," he continued sarcastically, "that Christ wasn't chosen by popular vote of the apostles. On the contrary – *He* chose *them.* And we, the hierarchy, as the apostolic successors, are charged with bringing the Good News of salvation to all humanity.

"If there is a problem, it can be found in our lax enforcement of Church doctrine, and not in our failure to listen to the complaints of malcontents!"

Before Fred could respond, the bishop left the hall. There was considerable chatter among the attendees.

The USCCB president, Archbishop Koys, banged his gavel for order:

"I am requesting Cardinal Whitaker proceed with his presentation. Please reserve any comments or questions you may have for the-question-and-answer period at the conclusion of his remarks."

Fred continued by explaining the structure and protocol of the project: the initial interviews at Old St. Pat's and Holy Name Cathedral; the preliminary email survey of 180 parishioners; the unexpectedly high email response; and the in-person interviews he conducted.

Fred then informed them:

"For this next phase, I need to analyze the email responses and the interviews, and determine the paramount issues. Based on that information, I will design a survey to go out to all parishioners in the Chicago Archdiocese and to interested former Catholics."

He told them about engaging Professor Barkley Sylvester, a noted psychologist and survey designer, to assist him. He brought up a slide of the same survey example Sylvester had used:

THIS COMPANY WELCOMES CONSTRUCTIVE OPINIONS FROM ITS EMPLOYEES.				
Strongly Disagree	Disagree	Neither Agree Nor Disagree	Agree	Strongly Agree
☐	☒	☐	☐	☐
THIS COMPANY SHOULD SPONSOR AN EMPLOYEE SOFTBALL TEAM.				
Strongly Disagree	Disagree	Neither Agree Nor Disagree	Agree	Strongly Agree
☐	☐	☐	☐	☒

"You can see the second question seems to be the most important in the eyes of the respondent," he observed. "But look what happens when we add another scale:"

THIS COMPANY WELCOMES CONSTRUCTIVE OPINIONS FROM ITS EMPLOYEES.

Strongly Disagree	Disagree	Neither Agree Nor Disagree	Agree	Strongly Agree
☐	☒	☐	☐	☐

Very Unimportant	Unimportant	Neither Important Nor Unimportant	Important	Very Important
☐	☐	☐	☐	☒

THIS COMPANY SHOULD SPONSOR AN EMPLOYEE SOFTBALL TEAM.

Strongly Disagree	Disagree	Neither Agree Nor Disagree	Agree	Strongly Agree
☐	☐	☐	☐	☒

Very Unimportant	Unimportant	Neither Important Nor Unimportant	Important	Very Important
☒	☐	☐	☐	☐

"This throws a totally different light on those two issues. The significance of the second statement pales in comparison to the first statement when we include a scale of 'Importance.' We feel the same kind of analysis will be useful in the survey for the Archdiocese."

When Fred finished, there was a question-and-answer session. There were few real challenges. It seemed Bishop Millard's earlier broadside had embarrassed those attending, and had given them no real appetite for a spirited follow-up. The few questions he had to field were substantive and rational.

"Will this initiative threaten the enforcement of Church doctrine," asked one bishop.

"No, Fred responded. "It should actually help, since it will identify areas of misunderstanding that need to be illuminated."

Another bishop expressed a concern that many in the room undoubtedly shared: "Will members of the hierarchy find their authority undercut?"

"Rather than undercut," Fred responded, "it will give them a unique opportunity to be proactive with the flocks they shepherd."

As Fred headed to the airport after the session, he reflected on the fact that the meeting was more successful than he had hoped it would be – definitely a good "dry run" for his presentation he will make to the College of Cardinals.

And he thought the extreme tirade by the bishop from Nebraska was actually a blessing in disguise. It managed to take all the oxygen out of the room, with the result that the question-and-answer session was civil, and, in his opinion, constructive.

CHAPTER 51

The next day, before he left home for the Archbishop Quigley Center, Elaine offered her help.

"Fred, you have a lot of work ahead of you with all those email responses. You're going to need help with the analysis for sure, and I am willing to ask for a leave of absence from the Muscular Dystrophy Association and lend a hand. Besides, keeping the project in the family will help assure the data and analysis remain confidential."

"I appreciate your offer, Elaine. However, Cardinal Rooney has made his executive assistant available if I need her, and he tells me she is efficient and reliable. I think I'll start with her, but I may need your help as I get more deeply into the analysis. I'm working in a very secure environment, I'm pleased to say."

Later, Fred arrived at his office in the Center and prepared to begin his analysis of the emails and interviews. He had read all the emails as they came in, and transferred them to a hard drive that Tim Schultz, head of the Archdiocese IT Department, had reserved for his exclusive use.

At the end of every day, this hard drive automatically backed itself up to a second hard drive. These storage drives were kept in a locked room. Only Fred and Tim Schultz's computers had access to them, so, along with Fred's password, the data was considered extra secure.

Fred booted his system, and transferred to the drive where his applications and files were stored. The monitor displayed the message:

CANNOT LOCATE WHITAKER PROJECT DRIVE

He tried to access the backup drive, and got a similar message. He closed the system down, and then rebooted it. Same results.

He called Tim Schultz in IT, and Tim came to his office to solve the problem. Stymied, Tim opened the locked room, checked the hardware, and found everything was connected properly.

He went back to his own desk, and with the password Fred gave him, entered the system from his own terminal. He ran some diagnostic tests, and discovered the hard drives had nothing on them.

"Cardinal Whitaker, there is nothing on your hard drive," he said with amazement.

"What do you mean 'nothing'?" Fred replied impatiently. "Maybe the directories somehow got trashed, but the data of course will be there. The directories can be rebuilt," he offered.

"Cardinal, there's nothing – no directories, no files, no software, no code of any kind – nothing. The drives are as clean as if they had never been used."

"That's impossible!," Fred gasped. "Everything was fine before I left for Philadelphia. Am I right that no one in the building has access to what I've been working on?"

'No one, Cardinal. The only exception for access are the technicians from Data Reliability Systems, a firm that periodically – about twice a year – runs reliability checks on all our software and hardware.

"Because of the complexity of our information schemes as they have evolved over recent years, this is our guarantee we won't face failures at some crucial time."

"Were they here while I was gone?"

"Yes, Cardinal. Two technicians, yesterday morning."

"Tim, call their office, and tell them what has happened."

In a few minutes, Tim returned, his face drained of color. "Cardinal Whitaker, I phoned DRS and they told me we are not scheduled for a reliability check until next month. They didn't send any technicians to see us yesterday."

Fred was stunned. But he did not panic. He was prepared.

***

"Elaine, you won't believe what happened today at the Archdiocesan headquarters," Fred stated as he came in from the garage.

"You've been nominated to be the next Archbishop of Chicago, but you turned it down because it doesn't pay enough!" Elaine guessed as she continued to slice the carrots.

"Seriously, what would amaze you?"

"At this stage of the game nothing would amaze me – nothing at all. I hope there hasn't been another tragedy."

"All my data is gone, totally destroyed. Two men impersonating legitimate technicians came in yesterday and wiped my data storage devices completely clean. Nothing's left. Nada!"

Elaine put down her paring knife. "My God in heaven, Fred! What are you going to do?"

"I was told from day one that, with my secure storage drive, plus a backup, I would have nothing to worry about. There's an old saying: 'Never say never, and never say always.' The perpetrators must have known I would be out of town."

"This is totally bizarre, Fred. What do these people want? What do they expect to get? What is driving them?"

"I wish I knew, Elaine. Power? Religious fanaticism? Fear? Some kind of revenge? Who knows?"

Elaine looked puzzled. "Why do you say 'fear'?"

"There may be some clerics," Fred explained, "who did things they were not proud of, and are worried their past actions will be exposed."

"And your data is gone!" It began to sink in. "What are you going to do?"

"My data is *not* gone, thank God! When the IT manager told me my files were 100% secure, I didn't believe him. Nothing is 100% secure!

"Every day that I received emails, I also made a copy on a flash memory device, and brought it home. I have two devices, and exchange them every day – a 'father' copy and a 'grandfather' copy. I haven't lost a thing!

"Elaine, this morning you offered to help me with the organization and analysis of the data. I no longer trust anybody. Is that offer still open?"

"Absolutely! I can take a leave of absence for a few weeks. Ever since the announcement that you were made a Cardinal, the staff at MDA has been riveted by the news about what you are doing, and the problems we have faced. The Executive Director made it clear that if you needed my help for awhile, it would be OK with him."

"I am going to arrange for you and me to have office space and a couple of computers at Kirkland & Ellis. I fully trust Albert Rooney, but I don't want to work in that building. We don't know where the staff members have their loyalties. I've discussed this with Rooney, and he understands and agrees."

"To start off with, we'll make an appointment with Professor Sylvester, and discuss next steps for the project."

CHAPTER 52

When Fred told Barkley Sylvester about the destroyed data, Sylvester held his face in his hands, and shook his head.

"I don't know what sort of crises you faced during your law career, Fred, but I can't imagine anything more challenging – and frightening – than what you have undertaken for the Church."

"The good news, Barkley, is it probably can't get any worse! It has only one direction to go, and that's up."

Sylvester had never met Elaine, and he shared with her some of his pleasant memories of teaching Fred, and working with him when he was a management consultant. Then they got down to business.

"You have redundant copies of the data – that's excellent. Without them, your project would be kaput. Your management and legal experience has paid off.

"Here's what you need to do. You must take each email, and isolate the issues the writer has discussed.

"Some writers will have expressed themselves in a crystal-clear way, and it won't be difficult to determine what is on their minds. Some, of course, won't, and you will need to read 'between the lines,' so to speak, to determine what they are truly saying, what issues are bothering them, what they really like or dislike about the Church.

"Does this make sense to you?"

"It reminds me," responded Fred, "of the dilemma I sometimes faced with witnesses in a court trial. There are some that appear to be evasive when they are examined, don't directly answer the questions presented to them, and I would need to probe and probe to get to the truth.

"They weren't necessarily obfuscating or being hostile. Often it was a case of not wanting to say anything negative, or perhaps hurting someone. I'm sure some of the respondents in the emails have real issues, but find it hard to express constructive criticism."

"You're hitting the nail on the head, Fred. It's human nature. Like Thumper the rabbit said in Walt Disney's *Bambi*, 'If you can't say something nice, don't say anything at all!'

"Once you have identified the issues and have expressed them unambiguously, then organize them into categories – four, six, perhaps more. One might be 'church governance,' another 'liturgy and theology,' and so on. Once you have done this, let's get together and talk about how to structure the opinion survey."

CHAPTER 53

The staff at Kirkland & Ellis had a warm welcome for the Whitakers. Everyone had followed the media reports from the beginning, and were terribly worried about their safety. They had all gotten to know Elaine over the years, and felt both of them were part of the K&E family.

Fred's former executive assistant Rachel was delighted to see him, and informed him with an ear-to-ear grin, "Mister Whitaker, we are redoing our office stationary, and you are being listed as 'Of Counsel' – should it read 'Frederick Cardinal Whitaker, Esq.?' "

Fred laughed, and shook his finger at her like she was a naughty child. "Don't even *think* of it, Rachel! Not only would it be poor form, but I truly don't know how long this gig will last. No one yet has told me I have a steady job!"

Their first day was spent in a lot of socializing, including with the managing partner, Joseph "Scotty" Campbell and the other senior partners. They all wanted to know whether there were any clues or leads that pointed to the perpetrators in this series of crimes, and regrettably Fred had to say "no."

"Those responsible have covered their tracts extremely well, and the authorities so far have come up empty-handed, I'm sorry to say."

Fred and Elaine were situated in a large office with two adjoining desks. They both had terminals and could work on data independently.

Fred loaded the software and the email copies from his flash memory. He couldn't think of a safer place he could be for data security, but he continued to make duplicate copies of everything onto flash memory devices, and they went home with him at the end of the day.

They spent some time doing an overview of the email, and the results of the in-person interviews, to get a feel of what they were working with. Based on what they saw, they came up with the following initial groupings for the data:

- *Church's Mission and Governance*

- *Sexual Misconduct of Clergyman*

- *The Role of the Laity*

- *Marriage and Sexual Practices of the Laity*

- *The Role of Women in the Church*

- *The Crisis of the Priesthood*

- *Married Clergy*

- *Church Membership*

- *Liturgy, Theology and the Sacraments*

As they were distilling the issues presented in the emails, Fred turned to Elaine, and said, "Sweetheart, I want you to read this one and tell me what you think."

She brought it up on her screen:

"I've had a lot of good experiences with priests during my life, but sometimes they are not as sensitive as they could be in dealing with parishioners. What really stands out in my mind is a priest – Father Thomas Costello – that was assigned to our parish many years ago.

"My 10 year-old daughter was a good girl, liked going to church and to the sacraments. After Father Costello had been at our parish for a few weeks, her attitude changed. She no longer wanted to go to Mass or to Holy Communion. She said she hated Father Costello, that he was a terrible man, but she would never tell me why she felt that way.

"She's an adult now, and has left the Church. Somehow Father Costello didn't know how to deal with children, and he embittered my daughter. Maybe priests should be trained better when it comes to children."

"What do you think, Elaine?"

"I think the child was molested, Fred. I believe the mother did not realize what was happening, or is afraid of actually accusing a priest of such a terrible thing. Why would the young girl not tell her mother what had happened, if it had not been molestation?"

"This email I think is a good example of the point Barkley Sylvester was making," Fred commented. "These messages have to be read very carefully – there may be more there than meets the eye."

CHAPTER 54

Fred and Elaine carefully went through the emails for the better part of two weeks, and recorded the issues under the proper categories.

Some respondents had only one problem or observation to communicate; most of them had several. And, of course, many related similar issues troubling them. Quite a few had no concerns at all, and wrote in praise of how their church was handling things.

It was time to begin Phase Three – the opinion survey itself.

Barkley Sylvester looked over the results of their analysis.

"This is a treasure-trove you have here – a good sample of what the people in the pews are thinking," he observed. "You should have no problem constructing a survey that will accurately reflect the issues of greatest concern to the majority of Chicago Catholics."

He put their list of issues on his desk, folded his hands on top of it, and instructed them:

"There are a few principles – certain guidelines – you need to follow in order to have an accurate and effective survey instrument, and also one that is 'user-friendly' so the greatest possible proportion of your target population will respond. That, of course, is key. Without a significant response, the validity of the survey can be challenged."

"What do you consider a good response should be?" asked Fred.

"On a survey of this nature, I wouldn't expect more than 50% to return the completed forms," Sylvester estimated.

"Some people never respond to surveys; some are too busy to give it consideration; and some couldn't care less about what the Catholic Church does – it's very low on their priority list. A response of one-half should be expected, and the results would be considered valid.

"You'll recall, Fred, I showed you an example of how each item on the survey should be worded as a neutral statement of fact – neither good nor bad – that the respondent can either agree or disagree with, and indicate whether he or she feels it is important or unimportant. Did Fred show that to you, Elaine?"

"Yes, he did, Barkley. He used that example in Philadelphia, and showed me the slide."

"Good. Next, keep in mind if you have two or three statements on the same subject, they should not be put together on the survey, or you may skew the results. Insert them at various places in the document, for instance, statement 2, 14, and 28.

"At the end of the survey, you should have a space where respondents can write any comments, statements or clarifications of their opinions and concerns.

"Finally, begin the survey with an explanation of what you are doing, and what advantage it is to the respondent to participate. That's part of being 'user-friendly.'

"Are you ready to have a go at it?" asked Sylvester.

"As ready as we'll ever be, wouldn't you say, Elaine?" Fred asked rhetorically

Elaine responded, "Let's go!"

CHAPTER 55

During his many trips to Chicago over the years, Monsignor Martin Ramsey had never stayed at The Drake Hotel.

No matter where he traveled in the country, Ramsey's first choice was always to stay in upscale hotels. However, until now, he had never made it to the elegant Drake. It wasn't just the ambiance that attracted him now. His meeting with Bishop Costello and Roméo Hayek would be at Hayek's condo, a short five-minute walk from there.

He preferred to visit Chicago in the fall, winter or spring, not in the summer. When he visited, he always made it a point to allow time for an evening at the Lyric Opera, and another, if possible, at the Chicago Symphony Orchestra. Granted summer usually meant better weather in Chicago, but it was the off-season for these two cultural treasures. He gladly tolerated the freezing-cold days of winter in the Windy City, if it ended with a beautifully performed operatic or symphonic masterpiece.

As recently as two weeks ago, this trip had not been on his calendar. However, he recently received another phone call from Cardinal Ruggieri, requiring him to come to Chicago now.

This time the call from Ruggieri was less agitated and rude – no slamming the phone in Ramsey's ear – but the tone of the message was the same, if not even more serious. Ruggieri's concerns demanded immediate attention.

Monsignor Ramsey needed to act.

The situation in Chicago is degenerating. Ruggieri is alarmed, and he wants me to personally intervene there. This won't be easy!

The morning after his arrival, he walked from the Drake to Hayek's condo. When he got off the elevator on the 23rd floor of the 880 North Lake Shore Drive building, Costello and Hayek greeted him. He had never met Hayek before.

"Good to see you again, Martin," Costello said, shaking his hand. "I wish, though, that circumstances for this meeting were different. This is definitely not the best of times. In fact, it may be the worst of times."

"Cardinal Ruggieri is distressed – to say the least - by the current situation, Tom. He's an amazing man – he seems to hear and know everything. His contacts are so extensive; they appear to be everywhere."

"He impressed us when we studied with him in Rome, Martin," Costello recalled. "Now, even more so."

"He's extremely disturbed," Monsignor Ramsey continued. "He knows Whitaker is continuing the Pope's initiative. None of the drastic attempts – by *someone,* I don't know whom – to stop Whitaker have worked."

"He's gaining momentum," Costello lamented. "Recently he gave an impressive presentation to the U.S. Conference of Catholic Bishops, despite some serious criticism. It seems nothing fazes him.

"Cardinal Rooney not only hasn't put the brakes on Whitaker – he's encouraging him! He's become part of his team! When Whitaker finishes his report, he'll go to Rome with Rooney at his side, supporting him. It can't get much worse!

"Martin, you know Ecclesia Vera Society members can't talk about their activities – after all, you made the rules – and I'm sure you're not asking us to. All I can say is we're doing all we possibly can to neutralize Whitaker's efforts. It's proving to be more difficult than you can imagine."

"Can I say a word or two, Padre?" Hayek interjected.

Padre? Ramsey looked at Hayek quizzically. Hayek continued:

"Me and my boys – the guys I count on – have given real good attention to this, you can bet. Whitaker's like a cat with nine lives. Somebody shoots up a church, but that don't scare 'im. Someone totals out his car, but he's not in it. He gets his data trashed, but he has a copy somewhere else.

"And you can't get near this guy – he's surrounded by a buncha lousy goons and they all carry 'heat.' What the hell can you do? If I could only sit down alone for a few minutes with this sonofabitch and – ah – 'reason' real good with him, then maybe . . ."

Bishop Costello jumped in before Hayek could embarrass him even more.

"Thank you for your observations, Roméo. We, of course, know about these things – like everyone, we have *read* about them in the newspapers. Martin, when you last spoke to Cardinal Ruggieri, did he have any suggestions?"

"He did. Since the bishops and cardinals are strongly opposed to what the Pope is having Whitaker do, even if he is successful in completing this survey and making a presentation to the College of Cardinals, Ruggieri believes he's not likely to receive a warm reception from them.

"However, Ruggieri thinks if Cardinal Rooney is by Whitaker's side and makes a strong defense of his results, then Rooney's enthusiastic endorsement could convince a certain number of cardinals to favor the results – cardinals, who would probably not support it otherwise. Ruggieri feels it's very important to keep the cardinals united in opposition to Whitaker.

"As an auxiliary bishop, Tom, you are part of Cardinal Rooney's inner circle, his Curia. Perhaps you, and some of your like-minded colleagues, can help him see the inherent dangers in what Whitaker's doing.

"If you can blunt Rooney's enthusiasm for the project," Ramsey stated more as a directive than a question, "it might encourage him to take action so Whitaker's project isn't concluded successfully.

"Are you willing to do this?"

Bishop Costello stared at the floor, slowly shaking his head. "This is a tall order, Martin. Once Cardinal Rooney has made up his mind, it's hard to change his direction. But yes, I'm willing to try to move Rooney off dead center.

"In the meantime, we'll continue to look for any chinks in Whitaker's armor we can exploit."

CHAPTER 56

Fred and Elaine sat down at their respective side-by-side desks at Kirkland & Ellis, and placed the pile of printed sheets before them – the fruit of their analysis of 182 emails and personal interviews.

They had identified about 400 comments, opinions, suggestions, complaints, praises, acknowledgments, grievances, accolades and a number of rambling streams of thought that defied classification.

Now came the hard part – how were they going to condense all this into an opinion survey?

"You lay out a format, Fred," Elaine suggested.

"I was planning to take my lead from you, sweetheart," he responded.

They looked at each other, shrugged, and began to laugh. Fred picked up some of the sheets, and thoughtfully rifled through them. Then he spent a minute or two reading the top sheet.

"Here's what we're going to do. Let's each take half of the pile, analyze each item, and translate it into a statement. Then let's note how many times certain issues are duplicated by the respondents. We should stop every once in a while to review what each of us is doing, to make sure we're being consistent, and refine the wording."

It was slow-going at first. There was a tendency to word the statements in such a way they telegraphed a need to "agree" or "disagree." They would catch each other doing this.

"Honey," Elaine commented on one occasion, "you wrote 'Marriage is sacred.' Who could disagree with that? What about something like 'Divorce should be allowed in the Catholic Church.' Don't you think that is more neutral, something that could be legitimately debated?"

On another occasion, Fred made this observation: "Elaine, I don't think you can say 'Bishops are never accountable for the sexual misconduct of the priests they supervise' without getting strong disagreement from almost everyone."

As Professor Sylvester had emphasized, any statement that wasn't a neutral observation had no place in this survey, and would prejudice the validity of the results.

They also had to determine which issues came up frequently. These issues needed to be stated several times in the survey, in different words, and dispersed among other statements.

Every morning and afternoon, they took a coffee break from this task that was proving to be both demanding and tedious. Often, they were joined by Rachel Fischer, who was fascinated by what they were doing,

"Anytime you need extra help," she offered, "let me know. We aren't that busy right now, and I'm sure Mr. Campbell wouldn't object."

Occasionally when they were struggling over how to word a certain statement, they would show it to Rachel, and she often came up with a good idea.

As Fred and Elaine's work progressed, the quality of their statements for the survey improved, as did their productivity. In six days, they had virtually completed their work on all the survey items.

At this point, Elaine told Fred: "Honey, I think it's time for me to get back to my job at the Muscular Dystrophy Association. I don't want them to forget I work there!"

"I understand," replied Fred. "Thanks for helping out. Your contribution has been significant."

Fred finalized the survey form (see Appendix), modified the one for former Catholics, and drafted instructions for both. He also wrote a cover letter for parishioners, and a separate one for those who had left the Church, even though he had not yet devised a plan as to how he would reach former Catholics. Both cover letters would go over his and Rooney's signatures.

CHAPTER 57

Albert Rooney went over the survey forms and the cover letters with Fred, and was highly impressed.

"You're asking the laity for opinions I've always taken for granted, Fred. In a way, after all these years, I'm afraid to find out what they're really thinking! But it's clear to me this is long overdue – by several decades, perhaps by a century. Our Church is bleeding – we need to find out why, and stem it!"

Rooney instructed Tim Schultz, the IT Center head, to provide Fred with a complete listing of the names and addresses of every parishioner in the Archdiocese, both in digital and print format. The names were grouped by parish and vicariate, though Fred wasn't planning to use that information.

"Albert, Tim has offered to handle the mailings, and any coding I may need. But to be honest, I'm hesitant to have any employee at the Archbishop Quigley Center involved. Tim may be completely trustworthy, but in light of the problems I've had, I am taking no chances. I hope you understand."

"You don't even have to explain this to me, Fred. I not only understand – I agree. You're doing the prudent thing."

Fred's next challenge was to gather demographic data. Although he knew the names of parishes and vicariates weren't relevant for the analysis, he knew their demographic make-up was important.

Barkley Sylvester put Fred in touch with a professor in DePaul University's Department of Sociology whose specialty was population data. He, in turn, gave Fred the names of appropriate contacts for demographic information at the offices of the City of Chicago, Cook County, and Lake County. These contacts provided him with an abundance of demographic data, much of it from the most recent U.S. Census.

Though the identity of the respondents was not relevant, Fred did need to sort the returns by age and gender, probable race or ethnicity, income levels, and geographic areas. All of these categories overlapped, but now he had the demographic information to do such an analysis.

However, that was easier said than done.

He turned again to his expert on survey matters – Barkley Sylvester – and hoped he wasn't dreaming the impossible dream.

"I've got the addresses of about two million Catholics in the Archdiocese and demographic information on the makeup of various neighborhoods," he related to Sylvester with a tone of frustration in his voice. "Now, how in hell am I going to know where the returned surveys are coming from without printing a code on the forms, and compromising my guarantee respondents will remain anonymous?"

"Believe it or not," Barkley responded with a slight air of smugness, "there's now a high-tech way of handling that problem."

"I know a printer – Condé Reproductions – with a computer program for what you need. As an envelope's address is printed, the survey for it will be printed simultaneously. The address will trigger the addition of an extra space between two words somewhere in the text of the survey, and then this particular survey copy will be stuffed into that particular envelope.

"It's all robotic – no human intervention at all."

"When the survey is returned, it will be read by an optical scanner, which will see this virtually unnoticeable aberration, and code it according to the part of the Archdiocese it came from. Anonymity is maintained, but the specific neighborhood will be identified."

Fred was relieved no code number needed to be stamped on the form that might make the recipient question their anonymity. Yet, the demographic information he needed would be available to him.

Now came an even bigger challenge.

✳✳✳

How many former Catholics were living in Chicago and the suburbs? It was estimated there were hundreds of thousands who used to be Catholics, but had left the Church for another denomination, or who now had no church affiliation at all.

Fred knew if these individuals could be surveyed, the feedback would be invaluable.

But how am I going to reach them?

He discussed the problem with Professor Sylvester, Cardinal Rooney, and Elaine. Among the group, there was consensus, and it was simple – *advertise* for them!

Fred was certain no ordinary advertisement would do. It had to be unusually clever, attention grabbing, and appealing.

In the past, Ogilvy & Mather advertising agency had been a client of Fred's at Kirkland & Ellis. Fred had good contacts there, so he got in touch with them. To his surprise, his survey for the Pope met their definition of a legitimate charity; they offered to do the work *pro bono*.

An ad campaign for local media was developed around the theme:

HERE'S YOUR CHANCE TO TELL
THE CATHOLIC CHURCH
WHAT YOU *REALLY* THINK!

The ads briefly described what the project was about, and how important the views and opinions of former Catholics were, not only to the Archdiocese of Chicago, but to the Pope. Both an "800" number and a website address were provided where one could request a survey form.

All the pieces for this phase of the initiative were now assembled. The ensuing days and weeks would determine how well they fell into place.

CHAPTER 58

Albert Rooney was stunned.

During my more than three decades as a priest and bishop, I've never seen or heard of a time when auxiliary bishops, en masse, have requested a meeting with their ordinary. It's the ordinary who calls the meetings, not the other way around!

Yet, Rooney's auxiliaries – the heads of his six vicariates – had requested a meeting with him. Something was afoot, and he assumed it had to do with Whitaker's project.

The request for the meeting was conveyed by Bishop Thomas Costello, who apparently was spokesman for the group. The meeting took place in a conference room at the Archbishop Quigley Center in the early afternoon.

Tom Costello was shifting in his seat, looking a bit uneasy. He looked around the room at his fellow auxiliaries, and they gave him a nod. He addressed the Cardinal:

"Your Eminence, thank you for meeting with us. It may be unprecedented for auxiliary bishops to request such a meeting, but there is something on our minds – something serious enough to prompt us to make this request."

His voice was slightly hoarse, and he poured himself a glass of water from a pitcher on the table, took a sip, and continued: "You may have guessed the object of our concern is the trajectory Cardinal Whitaker's project is following.

"He has sent out hundreds of thousands of opinion surveys to the faithful in our Archdiocese. He has also advertised in several media outlets, encouraging former Catholics to register their complaints – I probably should say, vent their spleen.

"None of this is healthy, Your Eminence. We would even go so far as to say it borders on being ungodly, even evil."

The other bishops in the room looked at Costello, and gave him nods of approval.

"Allowing this to happen in Chicago will establish a horrible precedent. It will produce a senseless domino effect worldwide – a tragic legacy for your pontificate. And we find including the opinions of former Catholics, those who didn't have the strength to follow the law of God, unconscionable."

Bishop Michael Cullen, Vicar of Vicariate IV, and Bishop Costello had agreed beforehand Cullen would speak next so it wouldn't appear it was entirely Costello's show.

Cullen was apprehensive.

Would this confrontation with the Archbishop have a dire affect on my career?

At the same time, he was certain resolving this issue was crucial for the future of the Church.

"Not only will this initiative convey the wrong message to the laity," Cullen emphasized, "but it will do irreparable damage to the authority structure of the Church.

"The laity has always accepted the guidance of the hierarchy, and Cardinal Whitaker's machinations will open the door to doubt and mistrust. He's already gotten the ball rolling, so you need to insist he let you review and edit his report before it goes to the Holy Father, so you can modify it, and mitigate the damage."

The other bishops nodded, almost in unison.

Cullen stopped there, and the room was silent.

Cardinal Rooney got up, and walked over to the window. He stood there, his hands clasped behind his back, looking out at the courtyard. After a minute or two, he turned around to the men sitting at the conference table, who were staring intently at him.

"How many of you are familiar with the Byzantine-Slavic Rite of the Catholic Church?" he asked.

The auxiliary bishops looked at each other with expressions of bewilderment, wondering where the Cardinal was going with this.

Not waiting for a response, Rooney continued:

"Saints Cyril and Methodius, as I'm sure you know, were apostles to the Slavic people in the ninth century, and adopted the Byzantine-Slavic liturgy especially for them, and even created an alphabet, named after St. Cyril – Cyrillic – so the liturgy could be written in Old Church Slavonic, a language these saints standardized. To this day, this is the liturgy used in many Eastern Rite Catholic Churches.

"Numerous Catholic priests are ordained in this Rite. Millions of Catholics throughout the world worship in the Byzantine-Slavic Rite.

"In this Rite, they have no rosary. They have many prayers which are different from the prayers we use in the Roman Rite. Their religious calendar is not the same as ours, and they venerate saints we do not venerate in the western Church.

"But they are disciples of Jesus Christ, just like us. They believe in the trinity, the divinity of Jesus, and His resurrection from the dead, just like us. They are Catholic, through and through, but the way they express their faith differs from the western tradition."

Cardinal Rooney returned to his seat, put his folded hands on the table, and visually surveyed the six prelates.

"We need to be sensitive to how the faithful need to express their worship, as society and cultures change over time. We've never taken a serious look at that need. And Pope Francis Xavier feels now is the time, and Chicago is the place.

"We also need to know why so many people have left the Church. If we had been more sensitive to their legitimate needs, would many of them still be practicing Catholics today?

"I can't answer these questions. But hopefully, we'll gain some insight as a result of this survey."

The members of this gathering were giving the Cardinal what can best be described as blank stares.

Rooney turned his gaze to Bishop Cullen:

"Mike, you raise the issue of Church governance. At the turn of the 20th century – almost 150 years ago – managers dictated directives to their employees, and their employees had no choice but to comply. Managers even dictated to customers, telling them what to buy, and the public went along with it.

"Times have changed. Management has become more collaborative with employees and sensitive to customers' needs. The Church hierarchy, though, continues to function the old way. Bishops are like managers, dictating to not only their employees, the priests, but also their customers, the laity. This model doesn't work in business. And, Mike, it isn't working in the Catholic Church.

'The hierarchy needs to stop making assumptions about what's best for the faithful, and find out what the laity really need, and what they are thinking. The truths of our religion will always remain the same, but we need to take a hard look at the way we present them to God's people.

"I'm conservative. I always have been and always will be. But is that the only way to go? I don't think so."

Cardinal Rooney thanked them all for coming, said he appreciated their frankness, and wanted them to know they had his full support. With that, he left the meeting.

The vicars remained for a few minutes, discussed what had just transpired, and then filed out.

Thomas Costello arrived at his office late afternoon. Shortly after his arrival, his phone rang.

"Welcome to Chicago, Cardinal Ruggieri! It's good to hear your voice. When can we get together? I have a lot to share with you."

CHAPTER 59

Just a few days after the mailings, the surveys began to trickle in. After the second week, the returns surged like a tsunami.

"Remarkable! – a 65% return! Much higher than I had anticipated," Barkley Sylvester noted enthusiastically. "This indicates a genuine interest in the purpose of the survey, and an optimism on the part of the respondents that the results of the effort will bear fruit."

Barkley clearly had adopted the project's objectives, as if they were his own.

"I am really amazed at the large number of former Catholics who responded to the advertisements," Fred added with comparable enthusiasm. "Over 11,000 – and 80% of them returned the forms!"

"The high return rate of completed forms from the former Catholics is really not all that amazing," Sylvester commented, "since all of the 11,000 had requested bring part of the survey in the first place."

The initial processing of the forms was easy. Opening the envelopes robotically and putting them through the optical scanner to determine demographic information, stamping them with the demographic code, reading the boxes marked with an "X," and storing the information electronically, was virtually automatic at Condé Reproductions.

However, the majority of the forms included hand-written opinions and comments at the end, many quite lengthy; and all those from former Catholics indicating which issues were key in their decisions to leave the Church, also had lots of other hand-written comments.

Fred needed Elaine's help again. The shear volume of surveys – over a million – with information that needed to be read and tabulated individually, was overwhelming.

"I won't have any problem getting another leave of absence, Fred. This project has captured our executive director's imagination – the goals we are striving for, along with the sacrifices we have made and the courage we have shown. Everyone at MDA is rooting for us!"

Fred hired his two sons, Bob and Chris, to assist (he paid them well, more than summer jobs would have paid). They were delighted to be part of this effort.

Keeping the work in the family was a way to ensure information would not leak out. But even more help was needed. Fred approached his former and reliable executive assistant, Rachel.

"I am flattered to be asked," Rachel responded with considerable excitement, "and really anxious to participate."

Kirkland & Ellis' management was happy to accommodate. Fred had his team in place.

***

Never in the history of the Catholic Church had such comprehensive information on the views of the faithful been assessed and compiled in such an organized manner. It took the entire summer of 2046, and most of the autumn, to complete the analysis of the hand-written data, and prepare it for digital entry.

Sylvester reminded Fred, "I have my own proprietary software to analyze opinion survey data that will factor in agreement-disagreement levels with important-unimportant levels to arrive at the true significance of the individual's response.

"It's a very powerful application, and will permit you to obtain all the information contained in the data, grouping it demographically and analyzing it on dozens of parameters."

"I'm not sure I communicated this to you before now," Fred informed Sylvester, almost apologetically, "but I'm also interested in the overall direction of an individual's frame of mind, as reflected in the way a person responds to several statements. This may prove to be significant information."

"That shouldn't be a problem," Sylvester advised him. "It is possible to combine the responses to more than one statement, if desired, to highlight the trend of an individual's – or group of individuals' – preferences and tendencies; for example: marriage issues, the sacraments, Church governance, or the role of women."

The task was awesome! Fred had almost too many choices of how to analyze the data. He did a few data runs, some of which were clearly not relevant, and others which were possibilities.

He discussed the parameters and results with Sylvester, Elaine, and Cardinal Rooney. Rooney was particularly helpful.

"Fred, let me tell you what someone, like me, who is responsible for the needs of a local church, would find beneficial. After all, it is the diocesan bishops who will need to act on the information, should this initiative go beyond a one archdiocese experiment."

As a result, over the ensuing weeks, Fred changed parameters several times, and spent many hours analyzing results, and attempting to relate the opinions, misconceptions – and yes, prejudices – of the laity in this very diverse Archdiocese.

He was finally able to make sense out of results that initially appeared contradictory, and to identify common denominators that at first seemed obscure. The hours of hard work by his team were paying off – thousands of hours spent tabulating, recording and analyzing the information provided by the overwhelming number of survey forms.

This gargantuan effort would culminate in the final phase of the project – preparation of the report with recommendations for the Holy Father.

CHAPTER 60

Fred devoted February and March to his final analysis of the data, and then began to prepare the report.

The results of every data run, which included all the survey statements and every relevant parameter, were attached as exhibits to the report. In order to make their meaning more apparent, results with logically related parameters were grouped together, and an explanation of each group's significance was included at the beginning. The exhibits ran 47 pages.

The report itself was 29 pages. A brief summary of the report's contents follows:

INTRODUCTION.

- *Purpose of the Report.*

- *Type of Survey Used and Rationale.*

- *Mechanics of Survey Construction.*

- *Techniques of Survey Administration.*

SURVEY OF THE LAITY OF THE ARCHDIOCESE OF CHICAGO.

- *Overall Assessment of Catholic Opinion and Attitudes in the Chicago Archdiocese.*

As evident from the responses to survey statements, and additional hand-written opinions and comments, Catholics in the Archdiocese are favorably disposed toward the Catholic Church. They see many problems, but continue to believe Catholicism is their religious home.

However, many see no need to attend Mass every Sunday, or to follow other Church rules. This is even more prevalent with young adults, for whom the Catholic faith plays a more minor role.

Many respondents, in their hand-written comments, expressed their concern the Church was frustrating any growth in moral theology, especially when it concerns sexual morality. Those who identified themselves as teachers of theology, overwhelmingly asserted the Church, in fact, was thwarting theological speculation of any kind.

In their hand-written comments, many feel parish clergy are frustrated by Archdiocesan leadership. They feel priests, but not laity, should have a say in the selection of their bishops.

- *Selected Opinion Statements with Significant Implications for Chicago Catholics.*

  - A majority does not feel their involvement in parish life is adequately appreciated by the clergy.

  - Most would like a say in the selection of priests for their parish.

  - Almost all feel contraception should be left up to individual couples.

  - More than half feel same-sex marriage should be permitted.

- Many conservatives feel left out by liberal trends in the Church.

- Most feel some sexual abuse of children by priests still goes on.

- Most support the ordination of women.

- Most feel abortion should be allowed, if it is necessary to save the mother's life.

- Most support a married clergy.

- Many are ambivalent about the Real Presence in the Eucharist, and the literal resurrection of Jesus from the dead.

- Most feel bishops should be held more accountable for the sexual misconduct of priests they supervise.

- Most feel the sacraments are important to them.

- Most feel many former Catholics would return to the Catholic faith if the Church reached out to them more aggressively.

- Many claim a significant motivation for going to Sunday Mass is to be with their friends.

• *Assessment of Catholic Opinion and Attitudes in the Chicago Archdiocese by Categories – Age, Racial and Ethnic, Income level, and Geographic area.*

• *Selected Opinion Statements with Significant Implications for Chicago Catholics by Categories – Age, Racial and Ethnic, Income level, and Geographic area.*

SURVEY OF FORMER CATHOLICS IN COOK AND LAKE COUNTIES.

- *Overall Assessment of Why They Left the Church.*

  The majority, by far, feel the Church is too doctrinaire, and has not made the changes necessary to be relevant in modern times. They feel clergy doesn't listen to the needs of the laity.

  Many became members of other Christian denominations they felt were less constraining, and a small number joined a non-Christian sect or religion. A significant number said they have no religious affiliation at all, but they, nevertheless, consider themselves spiritual.

- *Selected Opinion Statements with Significant Implications for Former Catholics.*

  - Many, if not most, share the same views on selected opinion statements as did practicing Catholics.

  - Most feel conservative priests and bishops are often out-of-step with the needs of the laity.

  - Many feel divorce should be allowed.

  - Most feel if the Catholic Church reached out more often to those who have left, many would return.

  - About half feel premarital sex is not sinful, if the man and woman truly love each other.

  - Almost half acknowledged the Mass and the sacraments are important to them.

SUMMARY AND ACTION PLAN.

- *For the Chicago Archdiocese.*

    It is apparent the issues between practicing Catholics and former Catholics are not great. The main difference is practicing Catholics still feel the Catholic Church is important to them.

    Since the issues are similar, one must wonder if some current Catholics may not be far from relinquishing their affiliation with the Church, and seeking out another religious institution.

    Paying attention to their issues seems critical to the laity. A concentrated effort should be made by the Archdiocese to create a mechanism for them to express what disturbs them, know it will reach Church leadership, and be given consideration. When their concerns regard fundamental articles of the Catholic faith, it may be a sign the Church is not doing a good job of communicating basic truths so these can be understood.

- *A Plan to Reach out to Former Catholics in Cook and Lake Counties.*

    The evidence noted above shows the issues of practicing Catholics and former Catholics are not dramatically different. The main difference is one group accepts the governance and magisterium of the Church, while the other does not.

The Archdiocese needs to establish a proactive outreach to former Catholics, making it possible for them to meet with appropriate laity, clergy and hierarchy, and voice their past and present concerns. This outreach should be supportive, compassionate, and non-threatening. Former Catholics should be assured their concerns are taken seriously, that the Church is going to address them in every way possible.

- *Broader Implications.*

This effort of communication and dialogue with practicing and former Catholics, if successful, could lay the groundwork for greater outreach to Protestant denominations, and to the non-aligned eastern churches.

Over the years, the Catholic Church has made ecumenical efforts with limited progress. One of the results from this local outreach initiative might be a more successful framework for a universal endeavor.

CONCLUSION.

We are convinced, by these results, that this process has been successful. We feel in the months and years to come, similar efforts should be undertaken in every Catholic diocese throughout the world. Local churches should then be given the autonomy to make appropriate non-doctrinal changes they identify.

The Holy See should consider establishing a congregation where the concerns of local churches regarding the universal Church can be reviewed on a regular basis, and suitable changes made, so the needs and desires of the greatest number of God's children worldwide can be addressed. Then will the Church fulfill St. Paul's aspiration, as expressed in 1 Corinthians 9-19 to "become all things to all men."

CHAPTER 61

This project – culminating in a document of 76 pages – had been underway for over a year. Everyone on Fred's team had made significant contributions, and even exceeded his expectations.

Two team members, though, played more significant roles than he had anticipated – Rachel and Chris.

Rachel was not a Catholic, not even a Christian. She was a Reformed Jew, and her father had big plans for her. He thought she was intelligent, articulate and principled – and should become a rabbi, just like he was.

"You know the Torah and other sacred Jewish scriptures almost as well as most young people who are studying to be rabbis," her father would tell her. "You have great promise, Rachel. Your faith means a great deal to you, and you always develop strong relationships with other people. The rabbinate needs young people like you."

Rachel truly hated to disappoint her father.

"Being a good rabbi takes much devotion and commitment, father. You are a wonderful role model. It's just that I don't have that calling. It's not what I'm supposed to do."

Sacred studies, however, honed her analytical abilities, and that, along with her intuition, were priceless during the reading and categorizing of well over a million hand-written opinions and comments.

In spite of her lack of a Catholic background, she quickly absorbed the issues involved, and could ferret out the true meaning of some of the most obscurely-written opinions, better than any one else on the team.

"You know, Mr. Whitaker, sometimes the issues Catholics have with their faith are not all that different from issues in Judaism. Not all Judaism is the same. There are Orthodox, Conservative and Reformed branches of our faith –one size does not fit all. And like the Catholic Church, many Jews have been drifting away from their religious roots."

This project was hard, and sometimes frustrating work, but Rachel was always upbeat, and kept her sense of humor. She loved the project – it was a nice break for her from the drudgery and pressures of her K&E responsibilities.

Fred wanted each team member to read the report, and voice any suggestions they might have. When he asked Rachel to review the report, she was flattered, and honored.

"This project has been a real eye-opener for me, Mr. Whitaker. It's given me an insight to the Catholic faith I couldn't have achieved any other way. All of us truly are so much alike! We have the same aspirations, and face the same problems. Thank you for enriching me with this opportunity!"

Fred obviously considered her an equal partner with the members of the Whitaker family. This inclusiveness was typical of Fred Whitaker, and she missed working for him since he retired from the practice.

Chris also played a unique role, which Fred had not anticipated. Especially when a respondent talked about the troubles a teenager was having with the faith, he could flush out the basic problem better than senior members of the team.

For instance, a parent complained about her son not having any interest in what was going on during Mass. Chris read the parent's other responses, integrated all this, and arrived at a conclusion:

"The priest is talking over the kid's head – the homilies are boring the kid. He thinks the priest is from another planet! I've got classmates in parishes like that!"

Fred's mission had a profound effect on the entire family, but especially on Chris.

He started out as a typical kid in his mid-teens – not taking anything too seriously, chaffing under parental supervision, and struggling with the emotions that come with having just discovered girls.

However, the impact of the church shooting, and the subsequent car bombing meant to kill his mother or father were profound. And then his father gave him a very grown-up summer job preparing data going to the Pope in Rome.

For better or for worse, these events were robbing Chris of his teenage years. Over the past 12 months, this boy had been forced to grow up quickly, and become a man.

"I'd love to write a term paper about what I did this summer, dad. There's not a kid in my class who could come even close to the story I could tell. The principal might actually have me make a presentation about this at a school assembly!"

Fred laughed. "And I'm sure I'd love to read that paper myself, Chris. However, we both know that's not possible – maybe after I make my presentation to the College of Cardinals."

Chris and Bob read the manuscript, and were pleased their dad valued their input. Elaine went over the document thoroughly, and had some syntax observations, which were helpful. She thought the report was excellent.

While Fred was analyzing the data and preparing the report, he had touched base with Barkley Sylvester several times. Sylvester had made suggestions as Fred progressed, so there were no real surprises in the finished product. However, after reading the completed report, he raved:

"I've read every word of the manuscript thoroughly, Fred, and went over the exhibits with a fine tooth comb. You have done an excellent job!"

Barkley Sylvester patted the final document lying on his desk a couple of times, gave Fred a big smile, and declared: "This document is going to knock the Pope's socks off!"

CHAPTER 62

The final team member to see the completed manuscript was Cardinal Rooney.

If you had told Fred a year ago he would consider Albert Rooney part of his "team," he would have thought it ridiculous, and totally impossible. Now, apparently, the only miracle, greater than Fred's being assigned this unprecedented analysis of Chicago's laity by the Pope, was the virtual conversion of Albert Rooney that followed.

Here was a man, traditional and conservative as any prelate in the Church, who now sees there must be room for more than one point-of-view, toleration for new ways of expressing one's faith, and a bigger and more inclusive tent.

Fred discussed – and marveled – at this remarkable set of circumstances with Elaine.

"Not only is he a team member, but he will likely play a significant role in selling my case to the College of Cardinals."

"It will be a tough sell," Elaine added, "but Rooney's a talented speaker, and he will grease the skids for you with this group – make them understand how important your work is for the future of the Church. I feel sure of that!"

Fred had an afternoon appointment with Rooney at the Archbishop Quigley Center to review with him the completed manuscript. Since he had kept the Archbishop up-to-date on his progress, he had already seen parts, but not the final document. Fred showed up with the manuscript in a small black briefcase, almost tailor-made for a document of this size.

After reading through the parts he had not yet seen, Albert Rooney sat back in his swivel chair, and smiled broadly.

"Fred, it's hard for me to adequately express how impressed I am with the results of your assignment! Nothing like this has ever been done before, not even attempted. I believe this marks the first day of a new era in the Church."

Fred responded with a well-justified sense of pride:

"If, as a result of this project, Catholicism becomes a richer experience for the faithful, and some former Catholics are motivated to take a second look at their decision to leave the Church, then all the efforts and sacrifices will have been worth it."

"I received a phone call from the Holy Father yesterday," Rooney continued. "Cardinal Patel has kept him abreast of your progress. He also knows of my change of attitude, that I now see and appreciate the importance of what you are doing.

"Francis Xavier wants you to send him a copy of your manuscript, and wants to meet with both of us in the near future. He is anxious to know what kind of presentation you are preparing for the College of Cardinals, and what my role will be. He also mentioned Stefano Paganelli, Senior Cardinal Bishop, is privy to this, and wants to assist in any way he can."

Fred interjected, "I believe your support before the College of Cardinals will be essential, Albert. There are undoubtedly some cardinals who are ambivalent, and will be swayed by your endorsement."

Rooney stood up, paced the length the room with his arms crossed and a look of concentration as if he was formulating his thoughts.

"Believe it or not, Fred, I now see the value of creating a new Order of cardinals – lay cardinals."

He returned to his chair.

"I don't visualize that change taking anything away from the Church hierarchy. On the contrary, I visualize this group of men communicating to Church leadership what the faithful are really thinking and needing, which will make the hierarchy more effective in their leadership roles. Lay cardinals can play the role of ombudsmen. Everyone will benefit, I think."

Cardinal Rooney leaned forward, and put his elbows on his desk.

"This is the message we need to take to the Holy Father. I am sure he will agree. And it is the program we must sell to the College of Cardinals. The Pope, of course, makes the decision to approve, but the cardinals, and the rest of the hierarchy, must make it work."

"Albert, I never thought we'd get to this point," Fred remarked with a broad smile.

"As you know, this has been a hard journey, for me personally and for my entire family. At the moment, I can only think of what Shakespeare said, 'All's Well That Ends Well.' You and I must get together, and work on our presentations for the Pope and for the cardinals."

"I was due to concelebrate a Mass tomorrow morning with Bishop Costello for a congregation of nuns in his vicariate, followed by a breakfast," Rooney confided, "but he called earlier today and canceled. He was vague. Said he had a conflict. Kind of strange, I thought, since we planned this weeks ago. The nuns were understanding, and we rescheduled the affair.

"So I'm free early tomorrow morning. If it would work for you, why don't you come by my residence about 8:00 a.m. We would have a couple of hours to plan a strategy and work on the details."

"That sounds fine," replied Fred. He put the manuscript back into the black briefcase.

"Why don't you take this briefcase back to your residence with you, and I won't have to lug it back to Evanston. It locks automatically when you close it, so let me give you the key."

"No need for the key," Rooney replied. "I won't be looking at it until you arrive."

CHAPTER 63

A cold front from the Arctic rolled out of Alberta into northern Illinois, and collided head-on with a warm front moving up from the Gulf of Mexico. Lightning lit the sky, accompanied with claps of thunder, as a mixture of sleet and freezing rain made driving conditions on Lake Shore Drive slippery and perilous.

On this March morning, Fred's SUV, with one of two security agents at the wheel, crawled south on Lake Shore Drive in heavy morning traffic, and took the North Avenue exit to the House of 19 Chimneys. The mansion wasn't the largest structure in the neighborhood, but it was imposing, taking on the visage of a gothic castle as sleet pelted the sides of the building, and bolts of lightning reflected ominously in its windows.

Chicago is a city with only three seasons – summer, autumn and winter. And the winter is interminable, sometimes continuing until late May or early June with only a flicker of good weather. And then, all of a sudden, it's hot and humid.

Fred laughed to himself as he remembered one day, years ago, when he was hosting a newly minted lawyer from the University of California Hastings College of Law, a potential candidate for Kirkland & Ellis.

After a day of interviews with the firm's partners, and strategy meetings at which the young man was included so he could see how the firm operated, Fred took him to dinner at The Signature Room At The 95th restaurant in the John Hancock Building.

Looking out one of the windows high above the city, the young lawyer commented, "You know, Fred, I flew in from the San Francisco late last night. It's mid-May, springtime in Northern California. This morning it was hot and humid. At lunch time we had a thunderstorm. Now it's snowing! Don't you have a springtime here?"

Fred, always seeing the humor in a situation, responded, "We had spring a few days ago. But I was in the bathroom and missed it!"

The agent drove into the circular driveway, and let Fred off at the stairs leading to the front door. He then went to park the car until Fred was ready to leave. Security always stayed with the car these days, never left it alone.

Fred ascended the porch stairs. As he reached the front door, he could hear loud screaming and wailing coming from inside. He reflexively reached for the doorknob, tried to open the door and it was locked. He rang the bell and then banged several times on the door.

Alana the cook unlocked and swung it open. She apparently had just arrived as she was still in her overcoat. "Oh, my God, Cardinal Whitaker! Oh, my God! Cardinal Rooney has been shot – I think he's dead!"

✱✱✱

"Where is Cardinal Rooney?" Fred demanded.

"In his den," Alana cried.

Fred rushed into the den, and there was Rooney, slumped to the side on his sofa, with a bullet wound in his chest. Fred felt for a pulse in his carotid artery, and there was none – he was clearly dead.

The drawers of Rooney's desk were open and papers strewn about the floor. Next to the desk was the black briefcase he had given him the afternoon before with the manuscript in it. The lock had been pried open, and the manuscript was gone.

Fred pulled out his cell phone, and dialed 911. Within moments, sirens could be heard throughout the neighborhood and a dozen squad cars with flashing lights descended on the mansion, along with an ambulance.

Shortly after, Chicago Police Superintendant Frank Ryan arrived, hardly surprising since the victim was the Cardinal Archbishop of Chicago. Fred knew Ryan from his days at Kirkland & Ellis when he was representing a defendant in a criminal case.

"Fred, this is most strange. There was apparently no forced entry. The Cardinal's wallet and watch were not removed. The gun that fired the bullet was held right next to is chest – there are powder burns to prove it. Cardinal Rooney was sitting on his sofa, apparently was calm. He didn't get up. No signs of a struggle. And amazingly, there is hardly any blood coming from the wound. This doesn't add up."

Alana was seated and still crying, but was no longer hysterical.

"Was anyone else supposed to be in the house with him this morning?" Ryan asked her.

"'Not that I know of, sir," she sobbed, with her face buried in her hands. "Usually Father Roszak, his assistant and master of ceremonies, who also resides at the mansion, would be present, but he is away on vacation. The Cardinal sometimes asks one of the auxiliary bishops to celebrate Mass with him in the morning, but no one was scheduled today."

"Did he say Mass?"

Alana got up and went to his chapel. On the altar was the chalice and a damp purifier, and there were cruets on the cruet table partially filled. "Yes, he did, sir," she responded.

Fred started to dial the Pope's phone number stored in his phone, but stopped, not knowing what effect this shock would have on him. So instead he dialed Cardinal Patel.

"He's in a meeting, Cardinal Whitaker," the person answering the phone told him.

"Cardinal Rooney has been murdered – I must talk to him now," Fred insisted.

In about 15 seconds, Sanjay Patel was on the phone. Fred told the stunned Secretary of State what he had just discovered, and that a copy of the manuscript had been taken. He described for Patel the strange circumstances of the murder scene.

"Are you familiar with the murder of Cardinal Christian Bauer about six years ago?" Patel asked.

"I've never heard of Christian Bauer," Fred replied.

Cardinal Patel described Bauer's murder scene to Fred.

"There are disturbing similarities, as you can see. And the investigation of the Bauer murder was incomplete. I suggest you relate this to your police superintendent, and request a blood sample be taken from Cardinal Rooney for analysis, and the wine and water contents of the cruets be analyzed."

"I appreciate the feedback from the Vatican's Secretary of State," Superintendent Ryan told Fred when he passed on Patel's message. "I have already ordered a complete forensic workup, since it is highly unlikely the tragic death of this churchman was caused by the bullet wound."

"There's an important manuscript missing," Fred informed the Superintendant. "It's obviously been stolen since the briefcase was forcibly ripped open."

Fred answered whatever questions the detectives had, as best as he could.

The media was out in force, held back by the yellow crime scene tape surrounding the property.

"Please don't talk to the media, Fred," Ryan requested. "With a crime like this, I want information coming only from my office."

Fred phoned Elaine at work.

"Elaine, the unthinkable has happened. We didn't think things could get any worse, but they have. Albert Rooney has been murdered! Please come home – the family has to be together now."

Fred called Chris' security detail, and asked them to bring him home from school. Bob was at Notre Dame, but he needed the rest of the family at home, safe and sound.

On his way back to Evanston, the first time he was able to quietly reflect on what had happened, Fred's emotions overflowed, and he sobbed, almost uncontrollably. The security agents expressed concern, but Fred shook his head and held out his palms with a "don't worry" gesture.

He rarely cried, and never sobbed. Until now.

CHAPTER 64

It was 3:00 p.m.. Fred Whitaker never has a highball before 5:00 p.m., but today he made an exception. Elaine joined him.

Great sadness over the death of Albert Rooney pervaded the three of them sitting in the living room. Profound sadness. And fear. Overwhelming fear. How could there be such evil powers inflicting suffering and death on good people? Indeed the world has always been that way, but how had the forces of evil found this little corner of the planet which they occupied?

Was this in fact the last straw? Fred reflected. *Regardless of the value this mission would have for the Church, was it time for me to send my manuscript to Rome, and call it quits? I retired to give my family more time and attention, only to end up demanding sacrifices from them they didn't sign up for. Maybe enough is enough!*

"I can tell your mind is churning," Elaine observed, breaking into Fred's contemplation. "I am worried about you and your safety and I know you are worried about the family. We've been through hell for over a year now, Fred. You have done a phenomenal job, against all odds.

"You are on the threshold of presenting your case to the most powerful man, and the most powerful body of clerics in the Catholic Church. You always win your cases, Fred. And you can win this one as well. It's totally up to you whether you see it through to the end. It's got to be your call. Whatever you decide, I will support you 100%!"

Chris had been quiet ever since he returned from school two hours before. No question the events of the past few months, not to mention the last 24 hours, had taken their toll. He was, after all, still a teenager, albeit a mature one, and was still learning how to sort out traumatic circumstances as they occurred in his life.

He spoke up: "Can I say a few words about this?" His parents nodded in assent.

"I know I'm not able to totally understand what the two of you have gone through. But I can tell you what I've gone through. A year ago you came back from Rome, dad, with this really great assignment from the Pope – it was unbelievable. I was really proud of you.

"Then there was the shoot-up of the church. Two days later, our car blew up, killing poor Tony Salera.

"I was really scared.

"After that, someone wiped out your data, but you kept going, The survey was successful, and mom, Bob and I helped you with the hand-written responses. Now it wasn't just *your* project – it was *our* project. If Bob were here, he would be saying the same thing.

"These thugs, whoever they are, killed poor Cardinal Rooney. He needed protection, but nobody knew it.

"You've got to continue on, dad, in honor of Cardinal Rooney. You always told me that, if I am doing the right thing, I shouldn't let anything or anyone get in my way.

"And you know our whole family is protected. The President of the United States should be so well-protected! We're going to be alright."

Chris struggled to find a metaphor to make his point. Then he thought of one from a movie:

"It's the fourth quarter, dad, and it's fourth down. The ball is on the five yard line. The Pope needs you, dad. You can score the touchdown."

Chris stopped, and looked at his mom and dad, who sat silently, staring at him. *Was I too outspoken? Did I say too much?* He slumped in his chair with his head bowed.

Fred got up and walked over to Chris. Head still down, Chris looked up at his dad over his eyebrows. Fred squeezed his shoulder. "You heard our son, Elaine. It's time for a touchdown!"

CHAPTER 65

A week later, the funeral Mass for Cardinal Rooney was held at Holy Name Cathedral, built in a Gothic revival style in the latter 19th century after the Great Chicago Fire. Rooney's coffin was placed at the front of the church, above which, dominating the sanctuary, was the strikingly exceptional *Resurrection Crucifix,* sculptured by Vivo Demetz for the Cathedral when it was renovated after Vatican II.

Every American cardinal was in attendance, as well as many other U.S. archbishops and bishops. The Papal Nuncio to the U.S. came out from Washington, D.C. The Holy See's Secretary of State, Sanjay Patel, was there as the personal representative of the Pope.

Attending as the President's representative was the Vice President of the United States. The Mayor of Chicago, the Governor of Illinois, and the U.S. senators and representatives from Illinois were all at the funeral Mass.

All the pews and chairs in the Cathedral were filled by invitation only. A number of spaces were reserved for Chicago's archdiocesan priests, distributed by lottery, and a section set aside for prominent members of the laity.

The Mass was concelebrated by all the cardinal-archbishops present; Cardinal David McLaughlin, Archbishop of New York, was principal celebrant.

The eulogy was delivered by Bishop Peter Dearhammer, a good friend of Rooney's who was an auxiliary bishop in Kansas City, Kansas when Albert Rooney was Archbishop there.

Seated in the sanctuary with all the other cardinals was Fred, who – for the first time – wore his red cassock and biretta which had been made for him in Rome. He felt awkward, and a bit out-of-place in the garments, but realized the symbolism was important for this occasion, and especially with this group of prelates.

After the funeral, there was the procession of cars, which followed the hearse carrying the body of Cardinal Rooney to the Mt. Carmel Cemetery in Hillside where he was interred in the Bishops' Mausoleum.

Chapter 66

The next day, Fred and Patel met for about three hours at Kirkland & Ellis. Since Rooney's murderer knew Rooney had a briefcase with a copy of the manuscript meant for the Pope, Fred began to suspect the Archbishop Quigley Center might be bugged and would not be a safe place for their meeting.

"Cardinal Patel, I want it clear I have no intention of being intimidated by these hoodlums, not after all my family and I have had been through. I will fulfill my responsibility, and see this project to a conclusion, a *successful* conclusion, I am certain."

He reviewed his survey findings with him and his thoughts of how he might present them to the General Congregation of cardinals.

Sanjay Patel beamed. He was impressed – overwhelmed is a better description – by what Fred showed him.

"My expectations for this project of yours were very high, Cardinal Whitaker, but you have outdone yourself! This report is truly a *tour de force*. No reasonable person could read this and find grounds to challenge your conclusions."

"You probably know," Fred added, "that over the years I have made a name for myself as a litigator – a good litigator. I've learned that when a case appears to be hopeless is the time you must redouble your efforts and pull out all the stops.

"I am not concerned about the Holy Father's approval of the findings from this survey. I feel confident that if he makes changes, they will be minimal. The real challenge will be to present a winning case before the College of Cardinals. That's my focus, and I am determined to achieve it.

"Here is a copy of my manuscript to take with you for Pope Francis Xavier so he can review it before my arrival in Rome."

"It's clear to me," Patel observed, "you are a man that, when his mind is made up, there's no stopping him! I admire you – no question you will succeed. Given what has happened in Chicago these past few months, however, my biggest concern is for your safety."

"I am as safe as humanly possible with our security detail," Fred advised him. "As my son observed, we are probably as secure as the U.S. President. I *am* worried about my security in Rome. And, I might add, my safety on the flight getting there."

"As far as Rome is concerned," Patel assured him, "you will have papal security personnel with you your entire time there. We'll see to that."

***

When Fred was informed that Patel would be in Chicago for Cardinal Rooney's funeral, he made an appointment for them to see Scotty Campbell, the managing partner at Kirkland & Ellis. He knew Campbell would appreciate this chance to meet the Vatican's Secretary of State. Further, he was sure it would be a good contact for Patel, since the Holy See might need K&E's international legal services at some time.

The three of them talked for over an hour on a broad range of subjects, including Fred's unprecedented mission for the Pope and the legal challenges the sex abuse scandals had caused the Church worldwide.

"Cardinal Patel," Campbell informed him, "in the past, our firm has represented the Holy See in legal matters, both here and in Europe. We remain ready at your beck and call whenever you need our services again."

They discussed, of course, the intrigue and violence Fred's project had precipitated. Fred talked about his anxiety regarding his safety on a flight to Rome.

"We have a client," Campbell informed Fred, "that owes our firm a great debt of gratitude, that money hardly can repay. In fact, I think his company is worth less than what he really owes us.

"He has an executive jet, a Gulfstream. He has offered to make it available for our use if we have an emergency need for it. As far as I'm concerned, this qualifies as an emergency. Besides, since it's for the Church, he can probably take a tax deduction for flying you to Rome.

"Here's what I suggest. As soon as the date of your meeting is set, let me know and I'll make arrangements. Rachel will make an 'official' airline reservation for you, which will serve as a smoke-screen. In fact, you won't be on that flight – you'll be on the Gulfstream and no one will know about it. That should provide plenty of security. How does that sound?"

"That sounds great, Scotty. Who will be my benefactor?"

"He owns the Streeterville Construction Company. His name is Roméo Hayek."

CHAPTER 67

Cardinal Patel Flew back to Rome the next day. Three days later, he phoned Fred.

"Cardinal Whitaker, we have dates for your meeting with the Pope, and for the General Congregation of the College of Cardinals for your presentation. Francis Xavier has read your report, and is very pleased with the results! He looks forward to his meeting with you to discuss them."

Scotty Campbell said he would call Hayek to request the Gulfstream be available three days prior to Fred's meeting with Francis Xavier.

Fred advised him that Elaine would not be coming with him.

"Needless to say, Scotty, none of the other cardinals have wives – at least, not that we know of! It would be very bad form for me to show up in Rome with my wife in tow!"

"Can I quote your whole statement *verbatim*, Fred," Campbell replied with a guffaw.

Campbell took special pleasure in providing the deception for Fred's departure, and thus helping him to complete his papal mission safely. He was a convert to the Catholic faith, and like many converts, he was devout and quite zealous.

He was very conservative in his practice of Catholicism, embraced the pre-Vatican II devotions, and preferred the Tridentine Mass in Latin. He used to joke that he became a Catholic because he liked the "smells and bells" – the bell-ringing and greater use of incense in the Latin Mass.

In spite of his traditional approach to Catholicism, he was very clear it wasn't for everyone, and he applauded the Pope's determination to find out what the laity was really thinking and feeling.

Later that day, Campbell came into Fred's office. "I spoke to Roméo Hayek, Fred. There is no problem. He is pleased to help out, and will have his jet available for you."

Rachel was plugged into this scheme, and Fred requested she make an airline reservation for him about eight hours after his departure time on Hayek's plane.

Finally, after more than a year of fear, almost insurmountable roadblocks, and terrifying challenges to himself and his family, he could see the light at the end of the tunnel.

The endless problems are behind me at last, thank God, and I'm going to bring this assignment to a successful conclusion!

CHAPTER 68

Four days after the funeral, Police Superintendent Frank Ryan called Fred at his Kirkland & Ellis office to let him know what their investigation of the crime scene had uncovered, and what the autopsy of Rooney's body had revealed. This information had not yet been released to the media.

"Whoever committed this crime was very careful, Fred. There are no fingerprints or other physical evidence that point to anyone. And the bullet wound to his chest did not kill the Cardinal – he was already dead. That is why there was almost no bleeding. Why he was shot at all is a mystery.

"He had a fair amount of sleeping medication in his body, not enough to kill him, but certainly enough to incapacitate him. We found the sleeping sedative dissolved in the cruet of wine he used at Mass. Somebody wanted to disable him before he was murdered.

"He died of a paralyzed heart. But nothing was found in this muscle that could have caused it to stop functioning. Our crime lab is excellent, but it is at a complete loss as to what caused the paralysis. We are sending samples of the heart tissue to the FBI Crime Lab, but our expectations are not great."

Fred was perplexed.

The terrifying gun shots at Immaculate Conception Church in Highland Park, the bombing of Elaine's car, the destruction of my computer files, the horrifying murder of Albert Rooney – all this must have been done by the same perpetrators. How could it be, in every case, the terrorists left absolutely no evidence behind, no trail the police can follow? It seems unbelievable!

"So you are saying, at this juncture, you have no evidence that might lead you to a suspect?" Fred asked the Superintendent in disbelief.

"I'm afraid not. We are still examining the crime scene. The Highland Park Police Department provided us with shell casings and bullet slugs from the Immaculate Conception attack, but nothing matches the slug taken from Cardinal Rooney's body.

"We interviewed all the auxiliary bishops he supervised, to see if any of them could have been there early that morning – remember, there was no forced entry – but they all have air-tight alibis. We caught up with his assistant, Father Roszak, to see if he was really out of town on vacation, and he was. We are at a dead end.

"We thought we might have a break-through, but it hasn't panned out. Around seven that morning, just a few minutes after the cardinal was murdered according the coroner, one of our squad cars saw a passenger vehicle leaving the circular drive in front of Cardinal Rooney's mansion. That isn't all that unusual, since it's a good place for cars to turn around.

"But at odd hours, if an unusual car is on or near the property of a 'mover and shaker,' we take the license number, if we're actually there to see it. Since this became a crime scene, we checked the license number, and it's registered to a company. We went to talk to their management, even met the people who had been in the car. It all seemed legit. They said they were in the area because they had a project close by; and in their line of work, they start pretty early.

"What was strange was the car – in their field, you'd expect to see something less fancy, but they drove a silver Mercedes."

Fred's face turned chalk-white.

*A **silver** Mercedes? Wasn't it a silver Mercedes that chased us home from church a year ago? How many people drive a silver Mercedes?*

"What's their line of work?" Fred asked.

"Construction," Ryan replied. "The Streeterville Construction Company."

CHAPTER 69

Fred had no more than hung up than he rushed down the hall to Scotty Campbell's office.

He told Barbara, Scotty's executive assistant: "I need to see Mr. Campbell – right away!"

"He's free, Mr. Whitaker. Go on in."

Fred plopped down in a chair opposite Campbell's desk. "Scotty, the water has just gotten very muddy."

He described the car chase from church with a silver Mercedes on their tail, and the silver Mercedes, belonging to Streeterville Construction leaving Rooney's driveway a few minutes after he was murdered.

"This may all be coincidental, Scotty, but given what's been happening, nothing seems coincidental any more."

Campbell stared at Fred for a number of seconds, then got out of his chair, and slowly started pacing the room, with his hands in his pockets.

Finally, he turned to Fred: "Shit, Whitaker, how did I ever get involved in this goddamned mess?"

Fred looked at him with a smirk: "I guess it's the luck of the Irish, Scotty."

"*Irish*, eh?" replied Campbell, and gave Fred a weak smile.

"Well, I *am* involved! You dragged me into your project, and there's no way in hell I'm going to let any SOBs, no matter who they are, get in the way of its successful completion. Two people have already paid the ultimate price. We're almost at the finish line. We can't take any chances. Let's be perfectly honest about this, Fred: you are a target – your life is in danger. Somehow we've got to get you to Rome – safely.

"Let's look at where we're at. You made a flight reservation for Rome, leaving next Thursday evening, just to throw the bad guys off, in case they wanted to injure you en route. You would have left that morning on Hayek's executive jet. Let's call that arrangement the 'double-cross.'

"Now Hayek and Streeterville Construction are looking like they may be part of the problem instead of the solution. It's time for a 'triple-cross.'

"Fred, do you have a good reason to go to Milwaukee at this time?"

"Yes I do. Milwaukee's Archbishop Roger Cunningham spoke to me in Philadelphia, and said, once the survey was completed, he wanted to talk to me about its implications."

"Call him. Tell him you are going to Rome on Thursday to see the Pope, and you wanted to talk to him on Wednesday morning before you leave. He'll surely see you. If he's unavailable, make an appointment with his next-in-charge, the Vicar General I imagine.

"Have your security detail drive you up, but don't go all the way to Milwaukee. You'll turn off at Mitchell Airport.

"Remember the Cessna turbo prop we own?"

"Of course I do. We used it for business around the country. I've flown on it several times."

"I'll see that it picks you up at Mitchell. It won't get you to Rome, but it will get you to LaGuardia. You'll take a taxi from there to JFK and board a flight to Rome. We leave everything else as it is – your reservation to leave O'Hare next Thursday evening, your plan to leave on Hayek's Gulfstream that morning. By Thursday morning, however, you'll already be in Rome.

"Don't say anything to anyone, Fred, other than Elaine. Don't tell your security people until you reach the airport turn-off – you don't know whom you can trust any more. Don't even tell the kids, lest they say something accidentally. We want to take no chances with this 'triple-cross.'"

"How are we going to handle the fact that I don't show up at Archbishop Cunningham's office? And what about Hayek and his Gulfstream?" Fred asked.

"Leave both to me," responded Campbell. "They'll be taken care of appropriately."

Campbell pushed a button on his intercom, and asked Rachel to come in. He gave her all the details, and asked her to make the arrangements. He told her Fred needed a "coded" reservation out of JFK.

" 'Coded' reservation sounds familiar, but I'm not entirely sure what it is," Fred acknowledged.

"It's an arrangement we have with certain airlines for international flights. They block out a seat for us but without a passenger name – then it no longer shows up as available in their reservation system.

"When the user shows up at the ticket counter, he or she gives the code number, and the passenger information the airline needs. In other words, the fact this particular passenger has a reservation is recorded just before takeoff time. When you are ready to leave Rome for home, phone Rachel and she will do the same for your return flight.

"Rachel, get Mr. Whitaker a cell phone in K&E's name. Fred, don't use your own cell phone for anything you don't want the world to know, in case someone has tapped it. Otherwise, keep using it normally so they don't know anything's up. Leave it home when you go to Mitchell Airport – you could be tracked by GPS. And don't talk to Elaine about these arrangements while you're inside your house, in case the house is bugged."

Scotty Campbell leaned back in his swivel chair, and gave a big sigh. "Well, I'm finished handling the hard stuff today. Now it's time to get busy with the easy stuff – my law practice!"

CHAPTER 70

Elaine was astonished – and shaken – to hear about a silver Mercedes intruding on their lives again, and greatly relieved that Scotty had created a solution to get Fred to Rome with almost no visibility. Not telling the kids was hard on both of them, but Campbell's reasoning made sense to them.

Fred phoned Sanjay Patel, using the phone Scotty had provided, to tell him when he would arrive at da Vinci, and the security measures they had devised. Patel told him a papal security team would meet him at the airport and bring him to Vatican City.

Since Fred was now arriving a day earlier than originally planned, Patel suggested that he, Fred, and Cardinal Paganelli meet at Patel's office the day after his arrival to discuss the findings he would present to the Pope the next day, and the script for the General Congregation session several days later.

"Stefano Paganelli is a highly effective speaker, and well thought of by most of the cardinals" Patel told Fred.

Sanjay Patel reflected silently to himself:

He's the one that "sold" the cardinals at the conclave on the importance of electing William Bracey as the next pope. He should make a significant contribution.

"I think he could be instrumental in selling the results of your survey to the other Cardinals."

When Fred called Archbishop Cunningham for an appointment the Wednesday of his flight, Cunningham was delighted.

"Im pleased and flattered you want to fill me in before seeing Francis Xavier," Cunningham responded with enthusiasm. "You must join me for lunch."

Fred felt positively lousy about lying to Cunningham, and using him as a pawn in this ruse. He was determined to contact him when he got home, and apologize. Hopefully, Scotty would say the right things to Cunningham on Wednesday when he canceled the appointment.

Wednesday morning, Fred kissed a tearful Elaine goodbye, and promised to take care of himself. She smiled, and with a twinkle in her eye, admonished him: "Be sure you brush your teeth twice a day!"

"You can count on that!," Fred assured her. "I packed some toothpaste – but now that I think about it, I'm not sure I packed my toothbrush." They laughed and hugged.

Eric Johnson with two other security agents drove Fred's SUV west on Dempster, and north on I–94 to the Wisconsin border. Then past the turnoffs for Kenosha and Sturtevant, and finally the exit ramp for the General Mitchell International Airport – a little over 80 miles.

"Turn here, Eric. Actually, I'm not going to see the Archbishop. "That was just a cover story, for security reasons. I'm boarding a Kirkland & Ellis airplane that will take me to another airport."

"I knew something was up," Johnson responded. "Why would you be bringing your suitcase for a short day trip to Milwaukee?"

Fred smiled, chortled a bit, actually. He thought he was not observed when he put his suitcase in the trunk the evening before. Since the car bombing and death of Tony Salera, nothing escapes the watchful eyes of Eric Johnson's team.

Thank God, he said to himself.

CHAPTER 71

Fred passed through Customs at da Vinci Airport, and was met by a man holding up a sign with the name "Whitaker" on it, similar to what limousine drivers do when they meet a client at an airport. This was a papal security guard who greeted Fred warmly, and led him out to a car with two other security people waiting.

They drove him to the Parco dei Principi Grand Hotel. This is where he and Elaine had stayed a year before. Fred found it comfortable – a familiar place, and some comfort in his life was very welcome now. The entire time he was in Rome, two security guards remained outside his hotel room, 24 hours a day.

Fred's arrival was mid-afternoon, and he was exhausted, not only from the trip, but from living on the edge for so many months in Chicago. He phoned Elaine at her office before he went to dinner.

"It was an uneventful flight, sweetheart, which of course is the best kind. I've got a security detail – everything's going to be fine. I went over my notes during the journey, and fully expect Patel, Paganelli and I will have a productive meeting tomorrow. Keep your fingers crossed!"

Fred had dinner at the hotel's Pauline Borghese, and retired early so he'd be rested for his meeting the next day.

The papal security team drove him to Vatican City in time for his 9:00 a.m. meeting at Patel's office. Cardinal Paganelli was already there.

"You can't imagine how much I have been looking forward to this meeting, Cardinal Whitaker," Paganelli said as he greeted Fred warmly. "I feel privileged the Pope and Cardinal Patel are including me as part of this historic and extraordinary event."

They spent the better part of the first hour talking about all Fred and his family had been through during the past year, and the other challenges he faced in completing the project.

"Over the millennia," Paganelli recalled, "since Christ gave Peter the keys to the kingdom, many women and men have sacrificed – have undergone horrendous sufferings and paid huge prices – for the sake of the Church and in defense of their faith.

"But you, Cardinal Whitaker," he continued with considerable feeling, "will find a place among the more courageous and dedicated disciples for what you have accomplished under the most dire of circumstances! I truly admire you!"

Fred expressed his appreciation for Paganelli's generous acknowledgement.

They spent some time discussing Albert Rooney, his tragic death, and the amazing conversion he had gone through during the mission – from an antagonist to an active supporter.

"There is a troubling similarity between Albert Rooney's murder, and that of Christian Bauer six years ago," Patel commented, the second time he had shared this observation with Fred. "As unlikely as it seems, it is frightening to think there might be a connection."

Except for an hour for lunch, they worked on the report, how Fred intended to present it to the Holy Father the next day, and also on his upcoming presentation to the College of Cardinals at a General Congregation six days later. Patel and Paganelli planned to be with Fred the next day when he met with the Pope.

"Francis Xavier is very supportive of your efforts," Patel reiterated to Fred. "When you meet him tomorrow, he'll mainly want to know how you plan to address the cardinals, what your emphasis will be, and what role he should play in the presentation."

They decided that Paganelli, after the Pope's opening comments, would introduce Fred, emphasizing the importance of this historic effort, and the value it will have for the Church.

"Stefano is an excellent orator and greatly admired," Patel informed Fred, causing Paganelli to blush a bit. "He is very convincing, and like you, a lawyer."

As a young man, Paganelli had been a litigator before he answered his calling to the priesthood. He had a Ph.D. in canon law, and had been active in the Holy See's legal system for many years.

"You don't want to overwhelm this crowd with an exhaustive presentation of your statistical exhibits" Paganelli advised Fred. "This will turn them off. What they need to see are the compelling trends highlighted in your report, and how this information will help them perform their roles more effectively.

"Also, during my introduction, I am going to focus on what the hierarchy has to gain from this initiative. Many of these men fear that giving a voice to the laity will threaten their clout as Church leaders. I will tell them 'not so' – I will put the lie to that."

"No matter how you look at it," Fred added, "getting this message across is going to be tough."

"I am convinced," Patel interjected, "that Francis Xavier will create a new Order of cardinals – lay cardinals – to bring the voice of the laity into the halls of Church governance, but not until the College of Cardinals has had time to debate the initiative, to digest it, and to accept its wisdom. That won't happen overnight, but it will happen."

They reviewed Fred's PowerPoint presentation, and agreed on some changes, given what they had discussed.

Cardinal Patel had made reservations for the three of them at the L'Archeologia Restaurant, opposite the catacombs on the old Appian Way. It was a pleasant and casual evening, with story-telling and much laughter.

"After our meeting tomorrow with the Holy Father," Patel observed, "we will have six days before the General Congregation.

Cardinals who aren't part of the Curia will be arriving in Rome from the four corners of the earth. I want to set up a few meetings for you with some of these men whom I believe are reasonably open-minded and could be instrumental in affecting the general tenor of the College of Cardinals."

Fred made the observation: "This sounds like the lobbying that goes on in Washington."

At the end of the evening, as they returned Fred to the Parco dei Principi Grand Hotel, Fred enthused, "This has been a truly remarkable day, gentlemen. I'm looking forward to our meeting with Francis Xavier tomorrow, and I'm very optimistic about the College of Cardinals presentation."

Fred turned to Paganelli. "Cardinal, you are a lawyer, and you know prevailing in court is a combination of good preparation, and a winning attitude. I think we have both going for us."

As he bid them goodnight, Fred expressed his confidence: "I feel we are part of an incredible epic – a watershed event in the history of the Roman Catholic Church."

***

Fred was up at 6:00 a.m. the next morning. He had a leisurely breakfast, and spent some time in his room, mentally going over what he planned to say to the Holy Father at the meeting, scheduled for 10:00 a.m..

He was upbeat, and excited. Despite the time difference, he called Elaine, waking her from a sound sleep to tell her about his feeling of exhilaration, and that, in spite of all the obstacles they had faced, it appeared that a success was on the horizon.

"No matter what roadblocks these malicious individuals construct, the Holy Spirit is still in charge, Elaine. I must continue to have faith in God, and in myself."

The papal security guards picked him up, and drove him through Rome to the Corso Vittorio Emanuele II, then across the Tiber, continuing on the Via San Pio X, and at the Via della Conciliazione they turned left toward St. Peter's Square.

About 150 yards before they reached St Peters' Square, where vehicle traffic was required to turn either right on Largo del Colonnato, or left on Via Paolo VI, they saw Carabinieri cars with flashing lights blocking pedestrians from entering Vatican City. Another 100 yards and traffic ground to a halt.

"Please let the Carabinieri know I have an appointment with the Pope, and must proceed if I am to be on time," Fred instructed one of his security guards. The guard got out of the car and approached the Carabinieri.

In less than a minute he came running back to the car. "Your Eminence, something terrible has happened – unbelievably terrible! The Pope is dead!"

CHAPTER 72

Sanjay Patel was about to leave for the papal apartments, when his phone rang. "Sanjay, I have some awful news – Francis Xavier has died," Cardinal Lusardi, the Camerlengo informed him in a grave tone of voice.

Patel was almost dumbstruck.

"What are you saying, Mario? What has happened?"

"The Pope was in his study, and had a heart attack. It was fatal."

"It was a heart attack?" Patel asked, struggling for words "Has a doctor seen him? Are you sure."

"I was called by a servant about a half hour ago. The Pope's doctor could not be reached. Fortunately, Antonio Ruggieri was with me, and as luck would have it, his physician, Dr. Amaro was there also. Within five minutes, we made it to the Pope's study, and Dr. Amaro declared him dead of a heart attack."

Cardinal Ruggieri's physician? He just happened to be there at the time of Francis Xavier's death?

The hair began to stand up on the back of Patel's neck.

"What sort of examination did he perform?"

"He said he could tell, just by looking at him. He said he's seen lots of heart attack victims. Cardinal Ruggieri added that Dr. Amaro always makes the right call. I am going to move the body to his bed for the traditional ritual."

"Don't touch that body, Mario," Patel demanded. "A coroner must see it right away, and there needs to be an autopsy."

"Don't tell me what to do, Sanjay," he angrily replied. "You know full well, with the Pope's death, you are no longer in charge. I am now the Acting Secretary of State. No Curia official during the *sede vacante* keeps his office except the Camerlengo and the Major Penitentiary. I make the decisions! Furthermore, an autopsy would desecrate the body."

Lusardi ended the phone call.

Desecrate the body! Patel reflected back on the outrageous comment made by Cardinal Kaufmann of Munich when an autopsy of the murdered Cardinal Bauer was requested. *What is going on here? Is this a conspiracy? How deep does it go?*

Sanjay Patel's mind was going a mile a minute. He needed to do something, and fast, before the body is embalmed and possible evidence destroyed. But what?

In a sudden flash of inspiration, it occurred to him. He checked his phone directory for the number of the Italian Foreign Minister.

Ever since his appointment as the Holy See's Secretary of State, Sanjay Patel had several productive contacts with Agostino Spallino, the Italian Foreign Minister. Patel found Spallino to be a straight-shooter with whom he could talk frankly. The affairs of the Holy See, and Italy, intersect at various points, one of them being capital crimes committed in Vatican City.

"Mr. Spallino," Patel addressed him, anxiety evident in his voice, "I think we have a possible murder at Vatican City, a high profile murder – no less than the Pope – and I think we must act quickly."

He gave Spallino the significant details that led to suspect a murder had been committed, including what had transpired in the U.S., and his fear that if they did not act quickly, valuable evidence could be destroyed forever.

Spallino recalled vividly the strange events surrounding the death of Christian Bauer, and that a Church prelate had blocked the performance of an autopsy.

'Hold on for a minute, Cardinal Patel, while I make a call on another phone."

In a few minutes, he was back. "There are Carabinieri in St. Peter's Square right now," he informed him. "Their commander has ordered them to enter the papal apartments, and to seal off the room where the body is located until crime investigators and the appropriate medical team arrive."

The Carabinieri demanded entrance to the papal apartments, and quickly arrived at the Pope's study, ordered everyone who was inside to leave, and sealed the entrance. They took the names of those whom they had expelled. One of them was Cardinal Lusardi, the Camerlengo.

"How dare you barge into the Pope's living area," Lusardi shouted at them. "His Holiness has died of a heart attack, and we need to prepare his body. Your interference is positively sacrilegious and shameful! Please leave the premises *now.*"

"Sir," the officer in charge addressed him, "this has been declared a crime scene, and no one will be permitted to enter until our investigators and medical personnel arrive for a full examination."

"I beg your pardon, officer," the Camerlengo responded indignantly. "Vatican City is an independent state, and I am the acting head of its government. You are violating our sovereignty, and I am ordering you to leave!"

The officer in charge walked over to Lusardi, stood right up close to him, looked him in the eye, and warned him:

"You will leave this area, sir, or I will have you arrested for tampering with the scene of a probable crime, for attempting to destroy evidence, obstructing justice and not obeying the legitimate instructions of an officer of the law performing his duty."

Lusardi and the others left.

CHAPTER 73

"Cardinal Patel, this is Agostino Spallino," the voice on the other end of the line informed him. "I am calling to give you some important information."

It had been three hours since the Camerlengo had reported Francis Xavier's death to Patel, and Patel had phoned Spallino. He had not left his office since then. He had been in deep sorrow over the death of the Pope and his good friend for many years. He had cried, and prayed. Sanjay was anxiously awaiting this call from Spallino.

"It is too early to definitively say what was the cause of death. But a doctor from the coroner's office has examined the body and found, on the chest, a large puncture wound, the kind a large needle would make if it had been forced into the heart. This was, beyond doubt, a murder.

"Until the autopsy, we won't know more. Our crime examiners are going through everything in the study to make sure all evidence is recovered. The Carabinieri wanted to check his appointment book to see who was supposed to see him prior to the murder, but unfortunately the book is missing. I am so thankful your intuition was keen enough to suspect the worst – the worst is exactly what happened."

"It is horrifying," Patel asserted, "to think the Pope's death could be related to Cardinal Bauer's death six years ago, or to the recent

243

murder of Cardinal Rooney in Chicago. But I'm sure that can't be ruled out. Do you have any plans to explore these possibilities?"

"Of course," Spallino responded. "Through Interpol, we are requesting all the information the FBI and the Chicago Police Department can supply us on Cardinal Albert Rooney's murder. We are also requesting the German government order the body of Cardinal Christian Bauer be exhumed and thoroughly examined for any evidence that still might exist on the true cause of his death.

"If there is a connection, it could be that the bullet wounds to the chest, suffered by Rooney and Bauer, may have been made to cover up the fact a lethal substance was injected into their hearts through the chest. Why else shoot a bullet into the heart of a dead man?"

"Speaking on behalf of the Prime Minister and of our government," Spallino concluded, "we offer our deepest sympathy, and that of the Italian nation, to you and the entire Catholic Church on the Holy Father's death at the hands of a vicious murderer. We will do everything in our power to pursue this case until the perpetrator is brought to justice."

When Spallino hung up, Sanjay had a sense of relief. The tragedy was still unspeakable. The pain inflicted on the faithful throughout the world would be felt no less intensely. The personal loss of his friend William Bracey would never go away. But he experienced the relief of knowing that responsible authorities were pursuing this unspeakable crime. The entire world would be watching, and the Italian government could not afford to leave any stone unturned until it had answers.

CHAPTER 74

Cardinal Patel suddenly realized that Fred Whitaker must have come for his meeting with the Pope, only to find out the Pope was dead. Where could Whitaker be now? In the crisis atmosphere that accompanied the tragedy, he had forgotten about Fred. He had a cell phone number for him, and must call him now.

After the shocking news that the Pope was dead, Fred was driven back to his hotel. He tried to phone Cardinal Patel, but was transferred to his voice mail, and the voice mail box was full.

He spent the next three hours, almost catatonic, watching the English language news on TV that, non-stop, covered the Pope's death, and then the report he had been murdered. Fred's cell phone rang.

"Cardinal Whitaker, I must apologize for not contacting you sooner. I hardly need to explain why."

Fred responded, "I am amazed you are even able to call me now. What an unbelievable tragedy!"

Patel went on to relate his conversations with the Camerlengo and then Foreign Minister Spallino, the criminal investigation initiated by the Carabinieri, and the aid that Spallino had requested from Interpol.

"I am sure you know the changes Francis Xavier's death has precipitated, Cardinal Whitaker – I should say 'Mr. Whitaker' now, since your appointment as cardinal ended with the Pope's death.

Every project the Holy Father has not yet officially approved no longer exists. Regrettably, it is as if none of the work you have done ever happened. There will be no General Congregation of cardinals to review it.

"The next Pope could resurrect it, but given the lack of support Francis Xavier received from the majority of bishops, it is unlikely the next Conclave will elect anyone nearly as progressive. This is sad."

"What should I do now, Cardinal Patel? Is there a role for me to play?"

"I'm afraid not," Patel responded. "In the eyes of Church leadership, you are no different than any other Catholic layperson in the world. Let me ask you: are the papal security guards still with you?"

Fred looked outside his hotel room door. "They are."

"I don't suspect that will last for long. As soon as the Camerlengo gets wind of your special treatment, he will withdraw them. In a day or two, for sure."

"We don't know what kind of conspiracy is going on, Mr. Whitaker. You must leave Rome as soon as possible, for your own safety."

"I will fly out first thing in the morning," Fred stated somewhat reluctantly.

How could it be ending like this?

"I would like to say that I look forward to working with you again, Mr. Whitaker, but it seems highly unlikely. Still, I do believe in miracles, and in Divine Providence. We will see what God wills. God bless you."

Sanjay Patel hung up.

***

Fred phoned Rachel at Kirkland & Ellis for a coded flight back to Chicago as early as possible the next morning. Since he continued to worry about his home phone being bugged, he asked Rachel to phone Elaine at her office, and give her the time of his arrival.

After an early breakfast, the papal security guards picked him up and took him out to da Vinci Airport. As they drove through he streets of Rome, and out to the Autostrada Roma - Aerporto di Fiumicino they would take to the airport, Fred began to reminisce about all that had happened to him during the last year and a half.

My selection by Father Sullivan and Cardinal Rooney to be the first lay cardinal, the meeting with the Pope, and the mission he mandated – it still seems unbelievable this really happened.

Then the troubles began – the car chase, the shooting up of a church, the car bombing resulting in the needless death of a security agent, Albert Rooney's realization of a more inclusive Church and how he paid for it with his life.

Still, there was much to be optimistic about – how the opinion survey went so well, how it revealed so much potentially important information for the Church.

How optimistic I was on the eve of my meeting with the Pope! And then – the unthinkable tragedy of Francis Xavier's murder.

Was this all for naught? In the final analysis, was this an exercise in futility? God only knows. That's literally true – only God knows.

He thought of Elaine whom he dearly loved, and without whose support he couldn't have stayed the course.

The sacrifices she had to make! The retirement plans she had to relinquish!

And his boys, especially Chris. Bob was at Notre Dame most of the time, but Chris was at home, and became an integral part of the drama. This teenager was wiser, and more mature, than other boys his age. His contributions to difficult situations were significant.

Fred vividly remembered the family discussion after Rooney's murder, when he was thinking of throwing in the towel and ending his involvement in the mission. He remembered what Chris told him, in his dramatic teenaged way of expressing himself:

"You've got to continue on, dad, in honor of Cardinal Rooney. You always told me, if I am doing the right thing, I shouldn't let anything or

anyone get in my way . . . It's the fourth quarter, dad, and it's fourth down. The ball is on the five yard line. The Pope needs you, dad. You can score the touchdown."

When I see Chris, he said to himself, *I'm going to tell him:*

"I couldn't score the touchdown this time, Chris. But I did the right thing – I did the right thing."

EPILOGUE

The people of every nation – Christians and non-Christians – were in a virtual state of shock. It was unimaginable – unthinkable – this could happen. Was it terrorism? Was it the act of a disgruntled subordinate? Where was the Pope's security detail? What happened to the Pope's missing appointment calendar? Who saw him on that last day?

Never in living memory had the Italian government pursued a criminal case with the intensity it now devoted to the investigation of Francis Xavier's murder. All divisions of the Carabinieri were involved – homicide, security, and antiterrorism. No lead was ignored; no stone was left unturned; no Vatican official, no matter how important his position, was immune to detailed scrutiny and interrogation.

From around the world, other governments offered to help with the investigation. Of special interest to the Italian authorities was the offer of assistance from Munich, Germany, where Cardinal Christian Bauer was buried, and from Chicago, where Cardinal Albert Rooney was murdered. Although the Italian officials couldn't yet tell the specific cause of Francis Xavier's death, they did find an unusual protein in his heart muscle. They wondered if this same protein was in the hearts of the other two men who died in a similar fashion. Could the three deaths be connected?

As the investigation continued with no closure in sight, cardinals from around the world converged on Rome to elect a successor to Francis Xavier.

"We thought the Church was at a crisis point when Francis Xavier was elected," lamented Stefano Paganelli, "but it seems to fade into insignificance in light of the catastrophe visited on Christianity with the brutal slaughter of the Holy Father."

Sanjay Patel, no longer Secretary of State with the Pope's death, was assisting the Senior Cardinal Bishop in providing hospitality, but primarily sharing sympathy and commiserating with the cardinals as they arrived for the funeral, followed by a General Congregation and Conclave.

"Besides attending to the needs of our brother cardinals," Patel informed Paganelli, "I'm still working to coordinate investigative efforts between the Vatican and the Italian government. Mario Lusardi, our illustrious Camerlengo, should be providing this assistance, but according to Agostino Spallino, the Italian Foreign Minister, he is more of a hindrance than a help in furthering the investigation, so I'm filling the gap."

Antonio Ruggieri, though no longer Prefect of the Congregation for the Doctrine of the Faith during the *sede vacante* period, was holding court – one-on-one – with many of the cardinals as they arrived in Rome.

This was not unusual. With upcoming papal elections in the past, Cardinal Ruggieri was noted for "subtly" campaigning for himself, attempting to win over votes of those who might be disinclined to support him – which was the majority of the electors.

Typically Cardinals came away from these devious arm-twisting sessions with Ruggieri, shaking their heads – sometimes bemused – sometimes annoyed – but rarely, if ever, converting to Ruggieri's cause.

"There is something different this time, Sanjay," observed Paganelli as they noted Ruggieri's very predictable modus operandi.

"I've spoken to a few cardinals after their meeting with Antonio. More than shrugging off the get-togethers as in the past, they appear to be seriously disturbed, and don't want to talk about it."

Patel thought for a moment.

"Maybe he's getting more aggressive in his approach. If so, this is a terrible time to do that. We all know human sensitivity is not his strong suit, but given the terrible tragedy we've been through, the last thing to win him votes is a ham-fisted approach on the eve of Francis Xavier's funeral. I'm sure that will backfire."

Francis Xavier's funeral was conducted in St. Peter's Square in front of the Basilica, where the funeral rites for Paul VII had been held less than two years ago. The number of secular and religious dignitaries attending set a new record, exceeding all expectations. Over 200 cardinals, almost the entire College of Cardinals, were present. Many of the infirmed cardinals were in wheel chairs, some with IV drips, and oxygen tanks to facilitate their breathing.

Presiding again at the funeral Mass was Federico Lanzillo, Dean of the College of Cardinals. His homily was a mixture of deep sorrow and praise, especially for Francis Xavier's courage in introducing "unparalleled innovations in his attempt to revitalize our Pilgrim Church."

Among the hundreds of Church dignitaries and secular leaders from around the globe who flanked the altar and coffin, and the hundreds of thousands who crowded the Square, there were few who did not shed a tear. Cardinal Lanzillo preached eloquently, and the liturgy proceeded in all its emotion-evoking beauty. Copious tears were shed when the Papal Gentlemen finally removed the coffin and carried it on their shoulders into the Basilica and down to the Grottos beneath, where the remains were interred.

After the funeral, the General Congregation dragged on for two weeks before drawing to a close. Observers were not surprised, since the issues facing the Church had clearly become more serious and complex in the intervening months since the last such gathering.

Two days after its conclusion, the cardinals entered the Sistine Chapel, in procession, for the Conclave.

Speculation as to who would be elected Pope was rampant – greater than ever before. Bishops and archbishops, media commentators, and the laity expressed a variety of reactions and opinions:

"The cardinals couldn't find one of their own to assume the leadership role last time. What will happen this time?"

"Who among the College of Cardinals has the courage to face the new challenges and potential dangers?"

"The laity throughout the world know about the survey in Chicago and will now have expectations. Will a pope be elected who can deal with those expectations?"

Media from around the globe descended on Rome and maintained an around-the-clock vigil outside the Sistine Chapel. Although always a major media event, this papal election – to choose the successor to a murdered Pontiff – riveted the attention of the entire planet. The Fourth Estate responded with minute-by-minute coverage. With even the first whiff of smoke emanating from the chimney above the Sistine Chapel – before it was yet possible to discern its color – regular programming was interrupted, TV cameras began to roll, and news anchors launched into breathless reporting.

The majority of pundits concluded this Conclave would be very long. The Conclave electing Francis Xavier had lasted for 11 days. As difficult as that choice had been for the cardinal electors, this time the circumstances made their task infinitely more challenging. Coupled with the fact the preceding General Congregation had dragged on for an exhausting two weeks, most observers thought this gathering would probably set a record as being the most lengthy in modern history.

The pundits were in for a surprise.

On the second day of the Conclave, the chimney above the Sistine Chapel began to belch white smoke. The bells of St. Peter's Basilica joyfully announced the good news. A two-thirds majority of cardinals had made its choice. The man who was destined to lead the Catholic Church into the second half of the 21st century – the man who would fill the Shoes of the Fisherman, who would occupy the Chair of St. Peter and guide the mourning and traumatized faithful during these difficult times to a new and brighter horizon – had been elected by the College of Cardinals.

The expressions of joy throughout Rome – and all of Christendom – were completely overwhelming. There was universal agreement that the terrible crisis in the Roman Catholic Church was coming to an end, benefiting not only Catholics, but all Christians. The short length of the Conclave made it clear the Cardinals had acted clearly and decisively to resolve it.

From all over Rome and its suburbs, tens of thousands of the faithful flocked to St. Peter's Square, joining those already there to be on hand when the new pope would be introduced from the Loggia of the Blessings balcony of the Basilica and give his blessing *Urbi et Orbi*. Authorities later estimated that over a million people crowded the Square and overflowed into the side streets.

Finally, the moment came. Walking out onto the balcony came the Senior Cardinal Deacon, accompanied by a small group of cardinals and, of course, the new Pope. The Senior Cardinal Deacon made the much anticipated announcement:

Annuntio vobis gaudium magnum! Habemus Papam!

"I announce to you a great Joy! We have a pope! Antonio Ruggieri, Pope Pius XIII."

Appendix

OPINION SURVEY

The Archdiocese of Chicago

OPINION SURVEY

Below is a series of statements regarding the Catholic Church, both in Chicago and in the world. After each statement are boxes where you can place an "X" ☒ to indicate you agree or disagree, and an "X" ☒ to indicate whether the statement is important or unimportant to you. Place just one 'X" to indicate your level of agreement, and one "X" to indicate the level of importance to you. The back of each sheet has the same statements in Spanish, if that is your preference.

If there is more than one adult in the house (18 years of age and older), please photocopy this form and have each adult fill out the survey.

Enclosed with this survey is a stamped, self-addressed envelope addressed to Frederick Cardinal Whitaker. Please mail the survey(s) in this envelope, or to Frederick Cardinal Whitaker, P.O. Box xxxx, Chicago, Illinois 606xx-xxxx.

This survey is anonymous, and totally confidential. No responders can or will be identified.

Your opinions are very important. Thank you for taking the time to share them with the Holy Father.

Please return the completed survey(s) by July, 15, 2046

MY GENDER IS: MALE ☐   FEMALE ☐

MY AGE IS BETWEEN: 18–29 ☐   30–49 ☐   50–64 ☐   65+ ☐

1. I HAVE A FAVORABLE VIEW OF THE CATHOLIC CHURCH.

Strongly Disagree	Disagree	Neither Agree Nor Disagree	Agree	Strongly Agree
☐	☐	☐	☐	☐

Very Unimportant	Unimportant	Neither Important Nor Unimportant	Important	Very Important
☐	☐	☐	☐	☐

2. I AM VERY SATISFIED WITH MY PARISH.

Strongly Disagree	Disagree	Neither Agree Nor Disagree	Agree	Strongly Agree
☐	☐	☐	☐	☐

Very Unimportant	Unimportant	Neither Important Nor Unimportant	Important	Very Important
☐	☐	☐	☐	☐

3. PARISHIONERS SHOULD HAVE A SAY IN SELECTING THEIR PARISH PRIESTS.

Strongly Disagree	Disagree	Neither Agree Nor Disagree	Agree	Strongly Agree
☐	☐	☐	☐	☐

Very Unimportant	Unimportant	Neither Important Nor Unimportant	Important	Very Important
☐	☐	☐	☐	☐

4. I RESPECT THE LEADERSHIP OF THE POPE, AND HIS TEACHING AUTHORITY.

Strongly Disagree	Disagree	Neither Agree Nor Disagree	Agree	Strongly Agree
☐	☐	☐	☐	☐

Very Unimportant	Unimportant	Neither Important Nor Unimportant	Important	Very Important
☐	☐	☐	☐	☐

5. DIVORCE SHOULD BE ALLOWED IN THE CATHOLIC CHURCH.

Strongly Disagree	Disagree	Neither Agree Nor Disagree	Agree	Strongly Agree
☐	☐	☐	☐	☐

Very Unimportant	Unimportant	Neither Important Nor Unimportant	Important	Very Important
☐	☐	☐	☐	☐

6. THE CATHOLIC CHURCH SHOULD ALLOW ABORTION, IF IT IS NECESSARY TO SAVE THE MOTHER'S LIFE.

Strongly Disagree	Disagree	Neither Agree Nor Disagree	Agree	Strongly Agree
☐	☐	☐	☐	☐

Very Unimportant	Unimportant	Neither Important Nor Unimportant	Important	Very Important
☐	☐	☐	☐	☐

7. CATHOLICS SHOULD HAVE A SAY IN SELECTING THEIR BISHOPS.

Strongly Disagree	Disagree	Neither Agree Nor Disagree	Agree	Strongly Agree
☐	☐	☐	☐	☐

Very Unimportant	Unimportant	Neither Important Nor Unimportant	Important	Very Important
☐	☐	☐	☐	☐

8. THE CATHOLIC CHURCH SHOULD SPEND MORE TIME LISTENING TO THE NEEDS OF THE LAITY.

Strongly Disagree	Disagree	Neither Agree Nor Disagree	Agree	Strongly Agree
☐	☐	☐	☐	☐

Very Unimportant	Unimportant	Neither Important Nor Unimportant	Important	Very Important
☐	☐	☐	☐	☐

9. SEXUAL ABUSE OF CHILDREN BY CERTAIN PRIESTS STILL GOES ON.

Strongly Disagree	Disagree	Neither Agree Nor Disagree	Agree	Strongly Agree
☐	☐	☐	☐	☐

Very Unimportant	Unimportant	Neither Important Nor Unimportant	Important	Very Important
☐	☐	☐	☐	☐

10. TRADITIONAL AND CONSERVATIVE PRIESTS AND BISHOPS ARE OFTEN OUT-OF-STEP WITH THE NEEDS OF THE LAITY.

Strongly Disagree	Disagree	Neither Agree Nor Disagree	Agree	Strongly Agree
☐	☐	☐	☐	☐

Very Unimportant	Unimportant	Neither Important Nor Unimportant	Important	Very Important
☐	☐	☐	☐	☐

11. THE CATHOLIC CHURCH SHOULD ALLOW ABORTION IN CASES OF RAPE.

Strongly Disagree	Disagree	Neither Agree Nor Disagree	Agree	Strongly Agree
☐	☐	☐	☐	☐

Very Unimportant	Unimportant	Neither Important Nor Unimportant	Important	Very Important
☐	☐	☐	☐	☐

12. MY PARISH NEEDS MORE PRIESTS IN ORDER TO SERVE THE NEEDS OF OUR PARISHIONERS EFFECTIVELY.

Strongly Disagree	Disagree	Neither Agree Nor Disagree	Agree	Strongly Agree
☐	☐	☐	☐	☐

Very Unimportant	Unimportant	Neither Important Nor Unimportant	Important	Very Important
☐	☐	☐	☐	☐

13. PRE-MARITAL SEX IS NEVER SINFUL.

Strongly Disagree	Disagree	Neither Agree Nor Disagree	Agree	Strongly Agree
☐	☐	☐	☐	☐

Very Unimportant	Unimportant	Neither Important Nor Unimportant	Important	Very Important
☐	☐	☐	☐	☐

14. BISHOPS SHOULD BE HELD MORE ACCOUNTABLE FOR SEXUAL MISCONDUCT OF THE PRIESTS THEY SUPERVISE.

Strongly Disagree	Disagree	Neither Agree Nor Disagree	Agree	Strongly Agree
☐	☐	☐	☐	☐

Very Unimportant	Unimportant	Neither Important Nor Unimportant	Important	Very Important
☐	☐	☐	☐	☐

15. THE ORDINATION OF WOMAN PRIESTS SHOULD BE PERMITTED.

Strongly Disagree	Disagree	Neither Agree Nor Disagree	Agree	Strongly Agree
☐	☐	☐	☐	☐

Very Unimportant	Unimportant	Neither Important Nor Unimportant	Important	Very Important
☐	☐	☐	☐	☐

16. BEING A CATHOLIC IS IMPORTANT TO ME.

Strongly Disagree	Disagree	Neither Agree Nor Disagree	Agree	Strongly Agree
☐	☐	☐	☐	☐

Very Unimportant	Unimportant	Neither Important Nor Unimportant	Important	Very Important
☐	☐	☐	☐	☐

17. THE CATHOLIC CHURCH SHOULD DO MORE TO ACCOMMODATE THE NEEDS OF ITS MEMBERS.

Strongly Disagree	Disagree	Neither Agree Nor Disagree	Agree	Strongly Agree
☐	☐	☐	☐	☐

Very Unimportant	Unimportant	Neither Important Nor Unimportant	Important	Very Important
☐	☐	☐	☐	☐

18. THE SACRAMENTS ARE IMPORTANT TO ME.

Strongly Disagree	Disagree	Neither Agree Nor Disagree	Agree	Strongly Agree
☐	☐	☐	☐	☐

Very Unimportant	Unimportant	Neither Important Nor Unimportant	Important	Very Important
☐	☐	☐	☐	☐

19. THE CATHOLIC CHURCH SHOULD PERMIT SAME-SEX MARRIAGE.

Strongly Disagree	Disagree	Neither Agree Nor Disagree	Agree	Strongly Agree
☐	☐	☐	☐	☐

Very Unimportant	Unimportant	Neither Important Nor Unimportant	Important	Very Important
☐	☐	☐	☐	☐

20. THE GOOD WORKS I DO IN LIFE ARE MORE IMPORTANT THAN WHAT I BELIEVE ABOUT GOD.

Strongly Disagree	Disagree	Neither Agree Nor Disagree	Agree	Strongly Agree
☐	☐	☐	☐	☐

Very Unimportant	Unimportant	Neither Important Nor Unimportant	Important	Very Important
☐	☐	☐	☐	☐

21. PARISHIONERS SHOULD HAVE A SAY AS TO HOW PARISH MONEY IS SPENT.

Strongly Disagree	Disagree	Neither Agree Nor Disagree	Agree	Strongly Agree
☐	☐	☐	☐	☐

Very Unimportant	Unimportant	Neither Important Nor Unimportant	Important	Very Important
☐	☐	☐	☐	☐

22. ABORTION IS ALWAYS SINFUL, AND SHOULD NOT BE ALLOWED IN THE CATHOLIC CHURCH.

Strongly Disagree	Disagree	Neither Agree Nor Disagree	Agree	Strongly Agree
☐	☐	☐	☐	☐

Very Unimportant	Unimportant	Neither Important Nor Unimportant	Important	Very Important
☐	☐	☐	☐	☐

23. PRIESTS SHOULD BE PERMITTED TO MARRY.

Strongly Disagree	Disagree	Neither Agree Nor Disagree	Agree	Strongly Agree
☐	☐	☐	☐	☐

Very Unimportant	Unimportant	Neither Important Nor Unimportant	Important	Very Important
☐	☐	☐	☐	☐

24. I BELIEVE THAT JESUS IS TRULY IN THE EUCHARIST, UNDER THE FORMS OF BREAD AND WINE.

Strongly Disagree	Disagree	Neither Agree Nor Disagree	Agree	Strongly Agree
☐	☐	☐	☐	☐

Very Unimportant	Unimportant	Neither Important Nor Unimportant	Important	Very Important
☐	☐	☐	☐	☐

25. IF THE CATHOLIC CHURCH REACHED OUT MORE OFTEN TO THOSE THAT HAVE LEFT, MANY WOULD RETURN.

Strongly Disagree	Disagree	Neither Agree Nor Disagree	Agree	Strongly Agree
☐	☐	☐	☐	☐

Very Unimportant	Unimportant	Neither Important Nor Unimportant	Important	Very Important
☐	☐	☐	☐	☐

26. THE CATHOLIC CHURCH IS NOT ACCOMMODATING THE NEEDS OF THE MORE CONSERVATIVE AND TRADITIONAL CATHOLICS.

Strongly Disagree	Disagree	Neither Agree Nor Disagree	Agree	Strongly Agree
☐	☐	☐	☐	☐

Very Unimportant	Unimportant	Neither Important Nor Unimportant	Important	Very Important
☐	☐	☐	☐	☐

27. IT MAKES NO DIFFERENCE TO ME IF A PRIEST IN MY PARISH IS GAY, AS LONG AS HE PERFORMS HIS DUTIES AND MEETS THE NEEDS OF THE PARISHIONERS.

Strongly Disagree	Disagree	Neither Agree Nor Disagree	Agree	Strongly Agree
☐	☐	☐	☐	☐

Very Unimportant	Unimportant	Neither Important Nor Unimportant	Important	Very Important
☐	☐	☐	☐	☐

28. PREMARITAL SEX IS NOT SINFUL, IF THE MAN AND WOMAN TRULY LOVE EACH OTHER.

Strongly Disagree	Disagree	Neither Agree Nor Disagree	Agree	Strongly Agree
☐	☐	☐	☐	☐

Very Unimportant	Unimportant	Neither Important Nor Unimportant	Important	Very Important
☐	☐	☐	☐	☐

29. WOMEN ARE NOT GIVEN EQUAL TREATMENT WITH MEN IN THE CATHOLIC CHURCH.

Strongly Disagree	Disagree	Neither Agree Nor Disagree	Agree	Strongly Agree
☐	☐	☐	☐	☐

Very Unimportant	Unimportant	Neither Important Nor Unimportant	Important	Very Important
☐	☐	☐	☐	☐

30. I RESPECT THE LEADERSHIP OF THE ARCHBISHOP.

Strongly Disagree	Disagree	Neither Agree Nor Disagree	Agree	Strongly Agree
☐	☐	☐	☐	☐

Very Unimportant	Unimportant	Neither Important Nor Unimportant	Important	Very Important
☐	☐	☐	☐	☐

31. THE ROLE OF THE LAITY ISN'T SUFFICIENTLY VALUED IN MY PARISH.

Strongly Disagree	Disagree	Neither Agree Nor Disagree	Agree	Strongly Agree
☐	☐	☐	☐	☐

Very Unimportant	Unimportant	Neither Important Nor Unimportant	Important	Very Important
☐	☐	☐	☐	☐

32. CONTRACEPTION SHOULD BE ENTIRELY LEFT UP TO THE COUPLE.

Strongly Disagree	Disagree	Neither Agree Nor Disagree	Agree	Strongly Agree
☐	☐	☐	☐	☐

Very Unimportant	Unimportant	Neither Important Nor Unimportant	Important	Very Important
☐	☐	☐	☐	☐

33. TOO MANY PROGRESSIVE AND LIBERAL CATHOLICS SEEM TO EMBRACE CHANGE FOR CHANGE'S SAKE, AND FORSAKE TIME- TESTED CATHOLIC VALUES.

Strongly Disagree	Disagree	Neither Agree Nor Disagree	Agree	Strongly Agree
☐	☐	☐	☐	☐

Very Unimportant	Unimportant	Neither Important Nor Unimportant	Important	Very Important
☐	☐	☐	☐	☐

34. THE MASS IS IMPORTANT TO ME.

Strongly Disagree	Disagree	Neither Agree Nor Disagree	Agree	Strongly Agree
☐	☐	☐	☐	☐

Very Unimportant	Unimportant	Neither Important Nor Unimportant	Important	Very Important
☐	☐	☐	☐	☐

35. FORMER PRIESTS, WHO ARE NOW MARRIED, SHOULD BE REINSTATED TO THE PRIESTHOOD, IF THEY WISH.

Strongly Disagree	Disagree	Neither Agree Nor Disagree	Agree	Strongly Agree
☐	☐	☐	☐	☐

Very Unimportant	Unimportant	Neither Important Nor Unimportant	Important	Very Important
☐	☐	☐	☐	☐

36. I BELIEVE IN THE RESURRECTION OF JESUS CHRIST FROM THE DEAD.

Strongly Disagree	Disagree	Neither Agree Nor Disagree	Agree	Strongly Agree
☐	☐	☐	☐	☐

Very Unimportant	Unimportant	Neither Important Nor Unimportant	Important	Very Important
☐	☐	☐	☐	☐

37. PEOPLE LEAVE THE CATHOLIC CHURCH BECAUSE THEY FEEL THEIR NEEDS ARE NOT BEING MET.

Strongly Disagree	Disagree	Neither Agree Nor Disagree	Agree	Strongly Agree
☐	☐	☐	☐	☐

Very Unimportant	Unimportant	Neither Important Nor Unimportant	Important	Very Important
☐	☐	☐	☐	☐

38. HOLY COMMUNION IS IMPORTANT TO ME.

Strongly Disagree	Disagree	Neither Agree Nor Disagree	Agree	Strongly Agree
☐	☐	☐	☐	☐

Very Unimportant	Unimportant	Neither Important Nor Unimportant	Important	Very Important
☐	☐	☐	☐	☐

39. HAVING AN ABORTION SHOULD NEVER BE CONSIDERED SINFUL.

Strongly Disagree	Disagree	Neither Agree Nor Disagree	Agree	Strongly Agree
☐	☐	☐	☐	☐

Very Unimportant	Unimportant	Neither Important Nor Unimportant	Important	Very Important
☐	☐	☐	☐	☐

40. I DO NOT ATTEND MASS EVERY SUNDAY.

Strongly Disagree	Disagree	Neither Agree Nor Disagree	Agree	Strongly Agree
☐	☐	☐	☐	☐

Very Unimportant	Unimportant	Neither Important Nor Unimportant	Important	Very Important
☐	☐	☐	☐	☐

41. I CAN THINK OF NO MAJOR ACTIONS THE CATHOLIC CHURCH NEEDS TO TAKE IN ORDER TO UPDATE ITSELF IN THE 21ST CENTURY.

Strongly Disagree	Disagree	Neither Agree Nor Disagree	Agree	Strongly Agree
☐	☐	☐	☐	☐

Very Unimportant	Unimportant	Neither Important Nor Unimportant	Important	Very Important
☐	☐	☐	☐	☐

271

(The following statement included only in the surveys sent to former Catholics)

In the space below, please indicate the numbers of those items that were most influential in your decision to leave the Catholic Church. Add any explanations, if you wish.

_____
_____
_____
_____
_____
_____
_____
_____
_____
_____
_____
_____
_____
_____
_____
_____
_____
_____
_____
_____
_____
_____
_____
_____
_____
_____
_____
_____
_____
_____
_____

(This statement included in the surveys for both current and former Catholics)

If you have any additional opinions or comments you wish to add, please write them in the space below. If you need additional sheets of paper, you may attach them to this survey:

_____

_____

_____

_____

_____

_____

_____

_____

_____

_____

_____

_____

_____

_____

_____

_____

_____

_____

_____

_____

_____

_____

_____

_____

THANK YOU FOR PARTICIPATING IN THE SURVEY

About the Author

Harry L. Sheehy is a former Jesuit with a keen interest in the role of the Catholic Church in modern society. With a BA and an MBA from Stanford University, as well as a DDS from Northwestern University, he has a diverse professional background that includes experiences as a business executive, a management consultant, health care provider, university professor, and liturgical director. He lives in Chicago with his wife, Carolyn.

The author of several creative nonfiction works, Sheehy wrote The People's Cardinal as his debut work of fiction. This suspense novel imagines the fate of the Catholic Church when the blind ambition of church leaders leads to perfidy and loss of their moral compasses.